THE MARS VINTAGE AND OTHER STORIES

A SPECULATIVE FICTION COLLECTION

ANITRA H. LYKKE

THE MARS VINTAGE AND OTHER STORIES

This is a work of fiction. All of the characters, organizations, locations and events portrayed in this collection are either products of the author's imagination or are used fictitiously.

Cover illustration: SelfPubBookCovers.com/SelinaMiyasia

Interior design: Vellum

Published by YMR Publishing, Kvitungevegen 26, 9100 Kvaløysletta, Norway.

www.ymrpublishing.com

YMR Logo design by: NEFERCHAU

ISBN 978-82-69-2344-0-4 (ebook mobi)

ISBN 978-82-69-2344-35 (ebook ePUB)

ISBN 978-82-692344-1-1 (paperback)

First edition.

Second impression.

For my mother Brit Heiberg, who loved that I wrote, but only got to read one of my stories.

FOREWORD

Traveling is a nice way to see other places, but living elsewhere and being forced to think in another dialect or another language is the real test. You are lead into the wondrous place where you see your own country, your people and yourself from the outside. I never quite could return to the mental place I once inhabited. That's probably why I love science fiction and fantasy.

INTRODUCTION

BY P. STUART ROBINSON

I'm wondering what is really appropriate to put in an intro-duction like this, being new to the genre... Should I mention we were in a writer's workshop together, which I founded (as luck would have it) with some rather attractive women who, I later learned, were also excellent writers? Probably not. I do believe that without said workshop and the author's consultation with yours truly, this collection might never have happened. Indeed, there's a case for crediting me as co-author – but that's a matter for my lawyers.

I see I'm falling into the trap (as usual) of wandering off topic and just writing about myself. Did I learn nothing from our lovely workshop! I will try and get back on topic at least, that is, the work herein contained of my dear friend and author, Anitra Lykke. Over the last few years, I've felt privileged to watch her craft evolve, hear her increasingly distinctive and authoritative voice, drawing us into each strange and wonderful tale. There's too much to say about this work, this voice, in such an introduction and in any case it's surely better to let the stories speak for themselves. A few thoughts will suffice.

There is a poetry or lyricism here, an elegance wedded to economy of expression. Like a painter's vanishing-point, strange worlds stretch out their alien tendrils between the lines, as real as any remorseless *implication* can make them. Such worlds to behold! And we get so much more than a peek inside! Prepare for full-body insertion into their alien logic, to be forced to think like 'them,' and question everything you've ever taken for granted. I was raised on science fiction. I suspect it is connected, perhaps by interstellar relay, to political radicalism, which I discovered lightyears later. Were we radical in our souls from the very start, or was it the serendipity of imagined futures and impossibly distant places that made us impatient with the imperfect here and now? Anitra Lykke and I may not be co-authors, lawsuits aside, but I like to think we are in some measure kindred spirits, with an urge to make a wish and a longing to make wishes come true. So, come all ye restless spirits! Settle down and, from the comfort of your armchair, let these stories spirit you away. You might change the world tomorrow but just now, in these pages, you can see how it might look – how it might feel!

P. Stuart Robinson, 2020

TRADE

Life was blissful and she was busy preparing for an unprecedented bountiful harvest season. The home-cloud was just thick enough for a perfect buoyancy and scents of the nourishing yellow-rain thrilled her children who had been more than willing to help out. She was really minding her own business, planning where to store the excess, but suddenly a shiny foreign ship appeared, with a long tube ending in a dark opening, and they were all sucked into it. The agony was excruciating, and she passed out.

She sensed confusion and concern, woke up in a container filled with a dense liquid, barely large enough for a family, and she was all alone. Her family was missing. Someone intelligent had done this! It was her job to organize everyone and fix things, but communication first!

"Who are you, and what do you think you are doing to us?" She said.

"Do you understand us?" The voice was audiosharp, but the complete meaning was still vague. She needed more information.

"Yes! Let us out again." Silly creatures.

"Intelligent beings should not be kept in containers."

"We are just trying to help you," it said. "We needed to put you in a pool." She moved towards a liminal area and eyed the moving creature up close. A weirdly quadropedic being with flat sunken eyes, clad in dark rubber and metal, looked back from the edge. It waved.

"Er, no. I am quite okay," she said. "Why did you put me in a box?"

"To save your life."

The pressure was unfamiliar and she felt so heavy. The gravity here was stronger than at home. She was elsewhere finally. But how?

"We come from another planet," it said, "far away."

"Well of course you do," she said. "You look far too strange to come from nearby."

"Hello, the creature said," and nodded its single head at her. "I am Mike."

"Hello Mike," she said. "I am mother." But it responded with a shudder and the scent of revulsion. Strange!

It began hammering on about how they knew it was strange, and that she needed to believe them.

"We know about other planets," she said calmly.

All right, so they came from a small dense planet further in-system, around the same star her own kind had lived in for generations. The planet didn't have a proper carrying life-sphere. She had never thought there could be intelligent life so close to a star, on such a small planet. It resembled one of the planets over at the next star, in a way. Just a hard shell with a thin layer of uninteresting gas-mixes. The creature felt and seemed sincere, its intentions mixed, but it was pleased with its own well-meaning attitude, it thought of itself as 'good people'. It claimed its ship had artificial gravity, but it was just spin.

One would think it and its kin could accommodate her needs, but they claimed she needed settings so low that it just wasn't possible. Their gravity was so enormous that her family's body-ship had almost flattened itself upon meeting their huge metal ship. An umbilical that was supposed to let them meet, squashed and sucked in her ship.

The lower pressure and the low artificial gravity in their guest-wing was trying on her body and made it hard to think clearly. Most of her family were obviously dead, and the other survivors were resting in a low-pressure pool, and preparing for the creation of a future and better adapted generation. She was the only one in the pool with one of the aliens, trying to communicate.

They were so coarse and hard-bodied, their sounds so loud, but she persisted. She had thought she didn't need a translator as she sensed their intentions more and more clearly, but there was a lot that was hard to understand anyway. They had such weird concepts, so she agreed to use their translator to see if that could help. They brought a hard, small box, but it hardly registered any senses, barely sound, and in a limited range at that. It also scrambled what little sense it did make, so she found it quite useless. The mike-creature in front of her wore a hard cover of rubber and glass over its protruding nose and small opening, but it had two more orifices available. Hurriedly, she designed, manufactured and excreted a better and softer device and swiftly attached it straight to one of its orifices.

The Mike screamed loudly: "Help!" and tried to remove the translator.

"It is not dangerous, it is a translating device," she said. "It helps me understand you."

The quadroped who called itself Mike stopped squirming and drew a deep breath.

Its pulse was much higher than before, but gradually it slowed down and started talking into a mouth piece, through both translators:

"Yes, all right. I will try to use your translator. Will you please not do anything without warning me first?"

"I did," she said, "I sent out warnings on all reasonable frequencies."

It spoke to some of its kin, and then brought its attention back to her.

"Yes, I see that you did, but it was not in any range we regularly use. Infrared, microwave, lots of signals," it said. "Can you please use this method we are communicating on now next time you wish to do something involving us?"

"Yes, she said." What limited beings they were.

It wanted to start all over. She obliged it, as if starting over in such a manner were possible, but it wanted to improve or impress. She let it assume innocence for now, but registered a non-warning type regular complaint of non-willful murder of a cross-species type, probable first contact accident, in case she needed it later.

"We are sorry for your loss," it said. "We didn't mean any harm. How are you feeling?"

"I am well," she said, "the water-taste is pleasant, even if the pressure is very high. I might not last very long."

The coming children would be better adapted, and she would program them to withstand a life at high gravity and high pressure.

She collected all her undulating parts, pulling in all her cilia, so as not to rip any more of them in contact with the Mike. She stretched out in a smile at it, and sent calming scents into the water as she said:

"You say you come in peace," she said and added sent scents saying: *Yet your kind killed most of my kin.*

Then she said loudly. "We come in peace." With the complement scent of: - *And we will kill your kin if we are not convinced of your innocence.*

"Welcome to Earth," it said.

She was not really sure if everything was being translated clearly and correct. The tastes were quite uncomfortable, but the being still seemed genuine. Why would it welcome her to their useless planet when they had brought her out in space? She was still in communication with others of her kind and the grand inter-world-network, but it was getting weaker. There was no relay nearby their planet. The Mike appeared to want something from her, but she didn't know what.

"We are looking for a planet to settle on," the Mike said.

"We are also looking to settle away from home," she said.

"Do you know of any other planets nearby where we could stay?" She asked.

A LONG TIME PASSED. The Mike exited the pool, and left her alone. Her children were almost ready to leave her. She swam into the pool with the rest of her even fewer kin. They agreed on a plan for the Mike's kin, and for their own.

The Mike came back and she swam to meet it and could again taste the rubber in the water. The Mike said:

"There is a planet we call the Morning Star. There is a high pressure on the ground, but we believe it is more to your liking high up in the atmosphere. Maybe you could live there?"

"What is it like, have you been there?"

"No, none of us in person, we just sent a few probes. The world Venus is too hot and to poisonous for us."

The Mike reeked of disgust, but there was also a wisp of a mind-image. Dissolving probes, of a kind that had not survived long.

She was not worried, acid was not the problem.

It stopped talking for a while. Then it moved away out of the pool through a portal. She could see it through the clear wall and hear it talk to another of its kind.

The Mike returned.

"If you want to live on Venus, you could buy it from us," it said. "We can even transport you there and we have checked, it is compatible with your biology."

"Is there other life on the planet?" *Acids/Prey/food?* It didn't understand her, or react. She tried again:

"Will we share this world?"

"No, it is pristine, it will be all yours." Then it shook all over. Another being came closer and they talked. Her translator picked up a new smell, an emotion: Humor or more likely eagerness. Then soberness overwhelmed it.

"We don't know it very well."

"We will think about it." Hm. She slowed down and thought about trade for a while. The Mike came and went as she did so. If she had a correct translation, that supposed the Mike's people owned it, and were allowed to sell it. How could you sell a world? But if they gave ownership to such large areas as a planet, what else was unfathomable about their culture?

Maybe it was neighborly to do as they did. She had always wished to travel further than her mother had, and did not really want to go home yet. She wondered how much they would like to get paid. But what would she do if the price was too high? Her prime directive was to not hurt any other intelligent beings, even if provoked, yet she wanted to get to know it.

If these beings had strange rules, she could at least try to follow them. She and her kin did need a new world soon, a place to expand. It would only take a few generations to adapt to this place, and fewer if the world was more like home.

What could she do about this situation in a peaceful manner?

Of course! She could just sell this planet they called the Earth, to the people on the next-door planet back home. That way she could pay the Mike for its morning star. Now, this idea seemed feasible. She wondered what they would say. If they were selling one world they couldn't use, then she could surely sell one she couldn't use yet. Her neighbors back home had a crowded planet, and with their hard, large bodies they would probably appreciate the place. She managed to access the relay and logged her willingness to sell, and her complaint against them. Then contacted her neighboring planet back home. They were elated as they had been searching far and wide without finding this little planet.

That seems improbable, they sent. *Too good to be true. Have you really bought a whole planet?*

That's how they do it around here, she sent.

Well, if it is true, we will buy it from you.

What can you pay?

They laughed delightedly, what an idea!

We can pay in radiation, mass or transport access.

How about a tiny black hole? She asked.

Don't you try! Restricted access to barbarians, you know that!

They laughed again.

Well, mass then, she sent, and specified the mass of the trade.

The contract was signed, and she brought her consciousness back to the pool, turned on her translator, and said to the Mike which was waiting eagerly:

"Yes. We want to buy the Venus planet."

The Mike left again, and talked to others of its kind for a time. Then it said:

"How much do you think you can pay?"

She laughed delightedly. She had understood them correctly and didn't need the footnote clause in the contract which negated it if misunderstandings had occurred due to language barriers!

"We can buy it, now that we can afford it."

"What do you mean?" It said, its confusion recognizable in the taste of the water.

"I have now sold your little planet, and since it has more volume and more mass, it would be more expensive than the Venus! We would like the rest paid in radiation, please!"

THE MARS VINTAGE

I had put everything I needed on the bed, my bag and I were almost ready for one more roundtrip to Mars. My shuttle was due to leave at midnight. Logan was a bit worried, but then my husband was always worried, usually about his vines, or about his herb-garden and now and then about my hitting an asteroid when I was out in space. He had fussed over me all day, and kept serving me tea, but now that I was almost done, he shouted something about a newsflash and disappeared into kitchen. I finished packing and zipped my bag. It deflated nicely into a compact flat shape. All I needed now was my phone, but where did I put it? Then I heard the familiar ring, a call from my company.

"It is a hell of a problem," my boss said. "How could you not have made sure you had all your permits in order?"

"I do," I said, and tried to remember when I had last checked them.

"No, you don't! Or do you have your permanent residential permit?"

"No, what kind of permit? Since when do I need one?"

"Since 1st January.

Haven't you been paying attention? It's all over the news right now!"

I really hadn't. Since I got back from my last haul, I had been so exhausted I had shut off all alerts, and just enjoyed a nice time with my husband. A month is not such a long time when you are having a holiday and helping out with the vineyard.

"It affects us all," he said. "We don't have enough pilots as it is, let alone any who can navigate the outer planets. We can't afford to have any more problems right now."

"I am sorry, but what is this residency-thing?"

"The problem is that as of tomorrow we're not allowed to have any outlander pilots anymore," he said. "You can't work for us, not anywhere in Earth-space."

It was a blow I had never anticipated.

"That doesn't mean I can't still work," I said, "even if my permit might be a bit late. Don't you think things will go back to normal in a few weeks?"

"Wishful dreaming," he snorted.

"Isn't there anything you can do?"

"It's not up to us, you just need to get this sorted."

I walked back into the kitchen and Logan was nowhere to be seen. I searched the house, then went outside where I could see his red hair among the vines.

"Logan," I shouted, "come on in."

He walked with heavy steps towards me, looking very glum. His long face showed how he hated my leaving for such long stretches of time. I used to love it, and love coming home, but it was getting harder and harder for me to leave, for both of us.

"Now what?" he said. "I thought you had left."

"Of course not. I never leave without saying a proper

goodbye," I said, "and now it seems I won't leave at all. Well, at least not tonight."

"What?" He looked at me, waiting. I felt like an idiot.

"There is a problem, I should have gotten a permit to stay here," I said.

"Really, why?"

"You didn't know either? There seems to be a new law, that requires people not born on Earth to have a residential permit."

"Since when? I haven't heard about such a thing since, oh I don't know when, since the history-books maybe, before unification and space-travel."

"I know. Evidently I should have had one since January."

"But didn't you get one when we married?"

"I thought so too, but since we are, don't you think they will let me be a legal Earthling pretty easily?"

He frowned, "We don't use that word," he said sternly. "We are Terrans!"

"Yes, of course. I have to apply to become a legal Terran immediately, or they won't let me work. Do you know how to do it?"

"I have no idea, but I can ask Sheryl, she's a lawyer." And I realized as I so often didn't, that my husband had a life of his own, outside our longish holidays when I was on Earth. When I was away.

"Sheryl, the pretty winemaker next door?" He gave me one of his looks. Don't go there, he signaled. But she was young and pretty, buxom even. Different from me in most ways, but a very nice woman. I had known her for years.

"She is both," he said, "these days, most people have two jobs, there isn't enough for her to do as a lawyer."

Logan went inside and called her, and I could hear him

arguing. She was my friend, but suddenly he seemed to know her a lot better than I did.

"How can Earth-Gov just decide to secede like that?" he said, then: "Yes, I know, but can you help? Come on over, we need to talk about this, so I'll cook something." The wrinkles on his brow had crept deeper into his skin when he came back into the room.

"She doesn't think it will be easy."

I logged on and checked my permits, and my boss had been right. There was a warning in the system, my license to pilot within the orbit of Mars was no longer valid, due to non-residency on Earth. How did they think that could work? Hardly any cargo travelled only between the outer planets. I lived my life in three places: On Earth with my husband and the vineyard in the warm climate of Scotland; On the freighter between planets, and on space-stations: Loading and unloading cargo. My birth-place Titan was just somewhere my parents lived, a more dangerous and tighter controlled society, yet someday I planned to take Logan to see it. Now I didn't know anything. If I had to choose, I would have chosen to stay on Earth, so I started the screen-work immediately. Where could I find anything? I searched the Earth-Gov site, and found a new official page, and tried sending an application for residency, which was automatically denied. What was this? I had to apply from outside the area I wanted to visit, what did that mean? All humans had always had access to all the planets and the moons in this system, as we all originated on Earth. Besides, I didn't want to visit. I wanted to live in my home with my husband. There was no option for that sort of application. And how did they plan and think it was possible to get out of the system to apply?

Gradually a wonderful scent wafted towards me from

the kitchen. Logan had started cooking, as he often did when he needed to think. I walked over and gave him a hug. He mumbled: "We have another problem."

"What?"

"My export-license was just revoked. I can't sell my wine outside Earth!"

"What? But.."

Sheryl walked in the door.

"Hi," she said, "I am sorry. This must be hard on both of you."

"Logan's wine is.." I began. He shook his head. That could wait. My license first. All right.

"Am I really in trouble?" I asked her.

"What," she said, "don't tell me you are one of the lazy buggers who forgot to apply for an Earth residency before it was too late?" She smiled, but her eyes were serious. We sat down, and when Logan served his wonderful stew, the comfortingly smell filled the old kitchen. I found a bottle and poured wine, not our own of course. I tried to enjoy it, as I never ate this well in space, where all food tended to taste pretty bland, but I couldn't focus. I told them about my application being denied. Logan cringed. The business was dependent on my good salary.

Sheryl had some important info.

"Even the usual temporary permits are being revoked," she said.

"Is it really that bad?" I asked.

"No appeal, I'd say that's pretty bad."

"Why is that, do you know?" Logan asked.

"How can they do this? It's not like we are at war!" I said.

"Aren't we?" She said.

I looked at her and felt the scoff fade on my face.

"No, not quite," she said. We ate in near silence.

"Tell me what happened," she said, when we had finished the first bowl.

"I came back from the Titan-run just before Christmas, as usual."

"Nothing was different?"

"No."

"At all? No unusual routines, no strange questions?"

I thought back. Had anyone said anything? Then I knew. I had seen something, I just hadn't connected the dots.

"There were separate entrances for Martians and Non-Martians on the space-station where I unloaded some of the cargo. It didn't affect me, but it was there. I think this might have started on Mars," I said.

"Why do you think so?" Logan asked, but Sherryl shook her head slowly, and I realized there was a longer story behind it.

"When was this?" she said.

"Late October."

"In November, I read that more and more politicians were debating the cost of *keeping the colonies*," she said.

Logan said: "Cost? Don't we get a lot of raw material from the outer planets?"

"Yes, most of what we, Terrans, need is mined outside Earth these days," I said. I knew because I transported a lot of it. "But the ones making money from it are on Earth."

The two of them had never been to space, so even if they were well read and properly educated, I needed to explain this thoroughly.

"The inner planets were all colonized by Earth, but most of the outer planets in our system were colonized by

Martian companies or by companies based on one of the Jovian moons, ok?"

They nodded.

"But since we were all part of one large political system, that didn't make much of a difference at the time. Our planetary system has always been one political unit, or everything would have become chaos, right? But, did you know that all the outer planets have at one time voted for independence?"

Logan looked shocked.

"No?"

"Well, they did, but until recently they all needed lots of supplements from Earth, so Earth could deny them their independence as just another silly matter, and ignore it."

Logan nodded.

"Because we could," said Sherryl and smiled ruefully. "A lot of people still think that everything in the planetary system is rightfully owned by Earth."

I shrugged. I had known people on Earth believed this in the old days, but now? Did Earth-Gov view all the other planets as colonies, not as equal members of a union?

"They needed the minerals from the rest of us, so Earth-Gov simply ordered that only members of the interplanetary union could have the vital supplements we needed." I understood the lingering resentment of that well, as we Titans knew all about needing something from Earth and only getting what they recognized as vital, no matter how much of our raw materials they were getting.

"How did you happen to come to Earth, anyway," Sheryl asked.

"I was sick of the grumbling about it at home and wanted to go see for myself when I graduated from pilot training."

"I never knew people on Titan wanted independence," Logan said. He talked, but I could see his mind was really elsewhere.

"No? Well, we were so far away that it didn't really make that much of a difference," I said. "The time-lag for news meant they were so out of date as to be irrelevant, so we just did our own things. On my first run to Earth I was so excited. No domes, just fresh air that anyone could breathe as much of as they wanted, and no terraforming scars in the landscape".

"Was Titan terraformed?" Titan was not that far away in terms of imagination, but the actual travel time was six whole months from Earth. Most Terrans had never been that far out. On Earth, it was considered adventurous to go to the Moon.

"Yes, of course, all the planets and moons where people live had to be terraformed, or we couldn't survive there," I said.

The lack of oxy-generators always humming in the distance scared me terribly at first, before I realized there was no need for that here, but I didn't tell them.

"I liked Earth," I said instead, "with the open spaces and free running drinking water. And I met my sweet Logan." He smiled at me, and Sherryl coughed.

"How was it back then?"

"Well, I got an in-system pilot job, but every now and then I had a cargo run further out." So, I had left Titan for a not so exiting routine-run between the inner planets and a new home on Earth. I was rarely back on Titan, but got some news from home whenever I had a delivery on Mars. Things tended not to stay so fresh on such a journey, even with hydroponics. No earth vegetables, and certainly no fresh news."

"But what did you mean, it all started with Mars?" Logan asked.

"Mars-Gov decided to limit the number of non-Martian humans allowed to study at Outer Uni," Sheryl said. I hadn't known that, but I knew their fancy universities were good.

"But they aren't as good as Oxford or Harvard, are they?"

"Mars Uni. and Outer Uni. are actually considered superior," Sheryl said.

"Outlanders," Logan scoffed.

"I have to admit the pilots from there are better, but still. I don't know about the others."

"What about wine and export?" Logan asked. "The news right now is bad. Export tax is really high these days, and...." He stopped.

I hadn't known about that either.

Sheryl and Logan started talking about the consequences for their wine-businesses while we cleared the table. I had made some raspberry- and gooseberry pies and put in the freezer for my dearest. Now was as good a time as any to serve one of them. I whipped up some thick cream and mixed it with a spoon of sherry, powdered sugar and finally chopped some walnuts to sprinkle on top.

It started as my problem, and they were already trying to figure out the disastrous consequences to our businesses. We all sat down with a screen each to check what could be done.

I remembered more from my last trip. When I had a few hours off at Luna space-station, near the moon, I had to pay a new air-tax. They said it had always been there, just under a different name. But now I wondered if it was for everybody, or just for all non-residents, including spacers.

The Moon had such a low gravity it got all the transit to and from Earth.

If reloading on Luna became more expensive, fewer Outer companies would bother to buy stuff from and sell to Earth. There were enough markets elsewhere. That meant fewer people could afford to import anything, and my cargo runs to Luna would dwindle. I checked the news again. A tourist company complained that the taxes on travel to Jupiter's moons had become prohibitively expensive, and were planning to drop them. Even so; For the Earth to leave the Sun-Union? To stop taking responsibility for humans everywhere? How could that work?

I found an entry I hadn't seen before: A research-group on Mars had recently managed to synthesize the vitamin supplements we all needed. I must have made a sound, they looked up: I told them, and I could see in their faces that they were understanding the implications: This was the missing important piece of information. For the first time in history, Earth didn't have anything vital that humans couldn't get elsewhere.

That would have to lead to severe changes in politics, and now it had. But why wasn't that being debated on social media and in the Newsflashes?

What Earth did have was our human heritage, and wine. Wine was my husband's thing. In particular: Scottish space-wine. Logan was in even more trouble than Sheryl, as his wonderful wines were all exports to wealthy space-cruisers and to the outer planets. On Mars, his wine was the only imported wine at all. He had no customers, and lots of competition on Earth. How could his winery survive this blow?

His superior grapes were specially gene-grafted and

blended to bear storing in space, and the cognac and wine containers we had developed together, were what gave him such a huge advantage in the export business. It had taken us years to experiment and taste our way to the perfect blend. It took so many trials to discover how the taste of the wine changed with weightlessness, how the taste altered with the recycled air and how all water-supply had its own flavor. Then we needed to find a way to counteract the problems, and design it. Space was one thing, but on arrival it changed even more, as the air-mix was slightly different on every space-station, and that affected how the wine tasted a lot.

Our most recent innovation however, was the new dehydration technique. Re-hydration at the other end saved enormous amounts of cargo volume and mass, and always affected the aroma, but it was easier to control. The right amount of Logan's special spice and our secret additives, tailored for each space-station and each planet, followed by local storage in our oak containers, recaptured some of the most wonderful Highland Reds, almost perfectly. His wines were perfect everywhere the air was recycled or reclaimed. The downside to all this, became evident today. His, or our wine, was barely drinkable on Earth with its wild and unpredictable air– and water flavor. And if he couldn't export it? Disaster.

I asked Sheryl what she would do.

"My vintage this year is quite good," she said, "and I expect yours could be changed into earth-based strains in a few years if you need to, but nothing is certain until everything settles down."

Logan sagged. He had just overcome the hardest years. The years of not knowing how well his inventions would work. Three years in a row his wines had won awards. He had just started to make more money than the developments had cost us. Then this.

"It says on the form that I need to leave, do you think they mean it?"

"I am afraid so," she said. "Will you manage?"

Logan looked at me. "We have the...," he said. I shushed him.

"Not yet," I said. "Besides, I am more worried for you, than for myself. I have moved planets before, I can do so again, but I don't really want to."

Sheryl looked at us both. "If you had children, it might have helped, - but only might, you see," she said. "And then only if they were under twelve." We ate slowly and finished the delicate pies with lots of cream. She left, trying to soothe my worries. "Good luck," she said. "You might be able to come back as soon as these idiots realize they can't do well without the rest of the Solar system. We'll be both isolated and in danger. It can't go on."

She was right. Logan asked me what she meant.

"Gravity," I said. "Any planet further out could lob large rocks into Earth atmosphere and kill everything, if they wanted."

He paled. "Really? I had no idea." I kissed him.

"Don't worry," I said. "I'm sure it won't come to that."

"And I will manage," I said.

"Of course, you will, but I am going to miss you so much, that I will probably get quite ill, and then where will you be? Not here to nurse me back to health." He was not entirely joking. It seemed I had to leave, if I wanted to or not. These days I longed for safety and stability more than the danger of my youth, and it was being denied me. We also needed the money, but if I left now, how could I be sure to be able to return? How could they leave people in troubles like that?

Unfortunately, my hasty application had made me visible to the authorities, and I was issued an exit-order the following morning. No time to put my life in order, maybe never to come back.

We walked silently around the house, talking, grieving. Hugging each other whenever we passed each other. He had work to do, but returned to the house after two hours. He withdrew a necklace and a ring from the safe, the ones with the purple diamonds he had given me on our ten-year anniversary.

"Use it to get back," he said. "If you can."

"No," I said, "you keep it, if you can't sell your wine, you need something to survive on. Or to visit me, when you can. I'll send money as soon as I can."

"I can always sell the vineyard to do that," he said. "Or grow carrots and soybeans instead."

The laughter stuck in my throat.

"Alright, I'll take the ring."

I also had a share in my family dome on Titan, but I couldn't really sell it to anyone outside the family group, and I couldn't do it from here. But I hoped I could live there, and Logan, if he managed the space trip with his awful claustrophobia.

"I'll join you when I have sold the farm," he said.

"Will you be able to?"

"I don't know, I hope so."

The last I did was a search to see if anyone else had had the same problem. Lots of sites had outcries from everybody who came from the outer planets. The Martians were especially colorful in their complaints, but there was no useful advice to find. I searched again in all the ways I could think of.

"What to do when stranded in a strange land," I said to the search engine.

Stranger in a strange land, came as a suggestion.

Contact your embassy was another.

I looked up 'embassy'. Aha. An office for just such a problem. I called them, even if it was 5.30 am. A very chipper voice answered.

"This is the Embassy for Saturn and Moons; how may I help you?"

"Yes," I said, "I am originally from Titan and..."

It interrupted:

"If your complaint is about a residential permit, we can no longer expedite such enquiries, please send an application to Earth-Gov"

"I have sent it...." I said.

"Please state your query," the voice interrupted again, as if it wasn't listening at all. The stupid AI was not doing its job.

"My application was denied," I said. "I need to leave today, but I don't have the right permits to leave Earth near-space, so I am stranded on Earth, and I am married here. Can you help?"

No answer, the phone was silent.

"And I wish to stay," I added. I waited. Some other voice said slowly.

"Do not attempt to leave or contact any other authority. Stay where you are. You will be picked up at 8. am."

My stomach knotted. Do not contact any other authority, like who? Like immigration? Like the police? Earth-Gov? Saturn-Gov? But I couldn't contact any of those except through the official channels. What did that mean?

Well, stay where you are, was fairly unambiguous, but did I dare do so? I felt like running. Then again, my implants lit up in any high-tech-environment, so I was quite recognizable as a human with implants, and even easier to find anywhere on Earth. I resigned myself to wait and see what happened. Logan and I stored everything of mine in the cellar, to be collected one day – maybe. If not, then Logan had access to everything if he wanted to. I was relieved I didn't have any children to have to leave behind. It was bad enough leaving Logan, and my things, and our house.

We went to bed, I clung to him, his beard tickling my cheeks and he held me like he would never let me go. I could not sleep, but lay there watching him when he fell asleep snoring now and then.

The noise from a hover-car woke me. How could I have overslept? My implant had given me no warning. But as I checked the time, I realized that I hadn't. It was still dark, only 5 am. I quickly dressed in my uniform and leaned over my sleepy, and barely conscious husband and said:

"They're early. I have to go. I love you."

"Bye, loveyou," he mumbled and his soft sleepy lips met my stressed tight ones.

Then his eyelids opened and he saw me, and kissed me passionately with his morning breath and all, and I softened, for a brief moment, in a way I hadn't felt in a long time.

"See you in a few weeks," I said, like I always did.

"See you soon," he replied as usual.

But nothing but the words were like usual. Neither of us said the ugly sharp words of *Goodbye* or *Never* aloud. I went downstairs with my flatpack and opened the door.

The car had landed on the gravel in front of our house, and the door slid open, not empty as expected.

A skinny man stepped out. Not my boss, or any copper or border-control-official, but someone I hadn't seen in eleven years.

"Hi, what are..," I started. He looked me straight in the face, very sternly and said:

"Get in, please!" I recognized an order when I heard it.

Okay, no kiss for old times' sake, or even a salute. So that was how it was going to be. I gathered my wits about me and realized that he was telling me about surveillance with every move of his body. I must be getting soft not to have realized earlier. I stored my flatpack in the secure door pocket and got into the spacious cabin with room for five, and a proper worktable. I slipped into space-force-mode and just nodded at him as he got in and sat down across from me. He nodded back and gave me a tiny smile with his eyes only. My implant suddenly worked again, and gave me his name, and his new position: Ambassador Solbit.

"Hello," he said more formally. "My name is Greg Solbit, I am the Saturn ambassador to Earth."

"Hello ambassador," I said, not a trace of irony in my voice.

He held up his hand to stop me saying anything more.

"Ms. Worth. Here is your travel itinerary, more information will be waiting at the spaceport, where you will be escorted out of the system."

Ms. Worth? Okay, so maybe I didn't have to pay for the trip at least, I had never been a Worth. The name I had used after I married Logan Worth was Dornworth. Then he gave me an id-card that linked to my implants, which surprisingly said: Elisabeth Dorn. Now this was better as far as I was concerned, my old identity was reinstated. I relaxed. He wanted me to use Ms. Worth for now, so Ms. Worth I was. Ms. Worth was an illegal alien on Earth, about to be transported back out of the system, whether that was to Titan or elsewhere I had no idea. But maybe not.

"Spaceport," he said to the car, and sat back in his seat. The harness closed across us, and tightened. Six point-belts, as if we would be flying in space. The car took off and we flew northwards, and I just sat there, waiting, looking out the window. The lush fields glinted green with dew in the morning light. I searched for a neutral topic, and realized I should ask what was going on, for whomever was listening.

"Why did I have to leave so suddenly? Can you please tell me what is going on?"

No answer.

"Have I done anything, or not done something I should have, apart from not applying for residency in time," I asked?

"It's for your own protection," he replied, and then said nothing more, however much I prodded. The car was silent, with excellent noise and vibration dampers. Grey and white, with black trimmings. Saturn division of spaceforce-colors. Suddenly the car swerved, and started plummeting. My stomach fell and I reacted instinctively, my implants overriding and taking control of the car, throwing up whatever passed for shields, righting the vessel and neatly avoiding a fast missile. I activated my helmet, but nothing else happened.

I cringed, a missile, here, on Earth? It had been too long since I did anything like this. Besides, the car reacted to me. It was no ordinary hover-car. I glanced over at the Ambassador.

"Did you just take over this car?" He asked casually after a little while.

"Sorry," I said.

He smiled: "Thank you!"

"Someone was shooting at us," I said. "Aren't you going to do anything about that?"

"Not right now," he said. "It was just a warning."

We passed Inverness and landed at the Scottish Space-port. He got up and looked around.

"Follow me," he said, and left the car.

I disconnected and followed.

We walked through the small spaceport, a port I thought I knew well. Past the train leading to *Domestic Air-traffic*, then past *Domestic Shuttles* to an exit I had never seen before marked: *Emigrations: Other destinations*. Not the International or the Interplanetary. Those exits were gone. When did that happen? Just a year ago everything was the way it had been for decades. It was empty, there were no guards and the shuttle looked like a regular Moon-ship.

The door opened into a blank room. He walked me inside, and for a moment left the door open. His phone pinged. He glanced at it, and said:

"I have a meeting I need to attend. Please wait here."

The door closed behind him. I waited.

When he came back he quickly closed the door, and unfolded and activated a handheld sound barrier.

"Now we can talk," he said. "Quickly! We need to leave soon. Earth-Gov is throwing out all outlander residents, all human residents, even the diplomats.

"Are they insane?" I asked, and realized this was huge, much more serious than my missing my husband for a while, and him not selling his wine anymore. Even though that was life-changing enough for the two of us.

"Unfortunately, they are not," he replied. "Just very self-serving and stupid."

"But throwing out even the merchants and the ones who make commerce happen?"

"Yes, and diplomats even."

"Did we need diplomats in the old days," I asked wistfully?"

"We have always needed diplomats," he said, "our kind have worked hard to avoid war for centuries. And they will soon discover that everything hangs together, things will gradually grind to a halt. Old technology will stop being repaired, new innovations will cease to happen all by themselves and the people will be very angry, so the politicians will lose their next elections, which will lead to..."

He stopped.

"But as yet, Earth politicians have voted to leave Sol-Union. To enforce it the way they want, they are getting rid of all critical voices, and all outsiders. Most left around the new year. Lots stayed on. Some didn't even notice."

"Like me."

"Yes. Lucky for me."

He glanced at the time: "We have ten minutes."

I asked: "What about my company?"

"What about it?"

"They said I wasn't allowed to fly for them anymore."

"That's right, I have requested you," he said.

"What?"

"This was the easiest way to do it. They were going to expel you without checking if your expertise was vital. It is. My Martian pilot was arrested on a trumped-up spy charge." He looked at me again, then asked:

"Don't tell me they forgot to tell you it has become dangerous to be a pilot?"

"More than normally?"

"Oh yes."

"Were you even asked to work for me?" He added.

"No," I said, "I was just told to stay where I was and expect to be picked up. I nearly ran," I admitted.

"Brilliant," he sighed. "All right. I'll have to ask formally. I'll not have it be said that I coerced anyone. Would you like to work for me as a pilot," he thought a minute, and added: "and occasionally as a chauffeur?"

I laughed: "Of course, but for how long?"

"For the duration," he said. "Six months? Five years? I have no idea, let's say for a year."

I could hardly believe my ears. A job. Near Earth even, to some extent.

"Pay?" He said. I waited expectantly, not daring to expect anything beyond my keep. But yet I hoped.

"Room, board and air, of course, and expenses, and... what was your previous wage?"

I told him.

"Exploitation," he growled. "I can easily double that. And bonus if we survive this."

"Why me?"

"Well, you do have a nice track-record, and no citizenship to lose on Earth, yet plenty of good reasons to not put people on Earth in any unnecessary danger."

"Thank you, I do need a job," I nodded.

He opened a door I hadn't seen and we walked towards a shuttle bay. Outside the entrance, we stopped: There were no guards there either, just a scanner in front of an airlock. I put my new ID to it, and he added that I was his new pilot.

"Suit?" I asked as the outer port opened.

"Your custom-made space-suit is waiting for you inside," he said, and we entered the slick little shuttle. The door closed. He went to the office-cabin and I sat down in the pilot chair and attached myself to the ship.

It was wonderful to be a part of a proper spaceship again. I could feel myself come alive. When I had accessed everything, I sent my dearest an encrypted message with my first paycheck:

I love you to the moon and back, forever and ever, or even all the way back from Mars. And I included a key only he would understand: *Where would I never drink your wine again?*

The worst place was, of course, on Earth.

ALL I NEED IS A SPACESUIT

Eoh, the grey airless moon had been my sanctuary, but as I came out of my studio that morning, I could feel my respite from the world ending. Bertha Sum, the meanest landlady this dome had ever had, stood in her doorway right between me and the padded outer door. Her short arms were crossed and she was not happy.

"You have to leave today, Eddie," the tiny woman said in a calm voice: "And take your bag of sewage, I shall need to fumigate everything after you've sullied my apartment."

Sewage? She couldn't be talking about my art, could she? I stopped to explain, but she had made up her mind.

"Please," I said. "You can't throw me out. You know it's freezing outside!"

"Watch me!" my landlady said with a sneer. I hadn't expected her to be that cruel, not today, of all days, when I finally had a new job.

"I am not worried. You have that fancy suit of yours, don't you?"

"But I need more than twenty-four hours of air, and my new job starts tomorrow!"

"Not my problem!"

What did she expect me to do? Sleep on the chilly streets, or if I wasn't allowed to do that, go *Outside*? My heater wouldn't last the day, nor my air. I'd be dead before my new contract even started.

When I fell out with my rich patron and lost my berth on his pleasure cruiser, I had to leave. They dropped me off here, but I certainly hadn't planned on staying on a moon with no art and no atmosphere.

Port authorities didn't know what to do with me, but as I got paid before the quarrel, and had sold the rest of my old sculptures on an earlier stopover, I had plenty of credits. I also had a shiny new spacesuit, so I looked more well-to-do than usual. When I agreed to place some credits in bond, they had directed me to the only other human on the moon.

I had found her tiny house with a lean-to studio in a shabby part of the main dome, situated close to one of the smaller maintenance exits. My awful landlady had welcomed me readily enough then:

"Welcome, my dear, I heard a human artist had arrived. How nice that you are coming to my home. We humans should stick together!" She meant humans with money, of course. I was the first human she had ever seen here, she said, as she offered me hot tea and a biscuit. It was heavenly good, and I accepted her terms without checking further. How stupid can you get! Then she set about to relieve me of all of my hard-earned credits. Now I was stuck here.

If not with my own trade as bio-sculptor, I had foolishly thought, I could earn my living as a designer or even a simple gardener, while I saved up to go look for my sister. But the Gobles who owned the moon had no use for a human gardener, they had machines to do that, possibly a lot better than I could.

I tried to grow a new batch of cell-culture in my dingy bathroom to make more sculptures, but she found out, and raised the rent. I hadn't really kept track of how much time had passed, as the local timekeeping was out of sync with the ship-time I was used to, and only loosely connected to the near-orbit-timeframe I grew up with, but it was probably six months or so. Money went fast when you had to pay for everything, even the air. Now I was out of money and out of cell-cultures to grow my beautiful sculptures. The weeks went by and no space-ship arrived in port, particularly not one that wanted a resident artist. We were too far from anywhere interesting, and the Goble's mining company was here for the minerals anyway, not the scenery.

My landlady was out of patience.

"You're two weeks behind", she said, "what did you expect, to stay for free?" I looked at her. I pawned the suit two months ago, getting just enough to pay for the room, and my habit of breathing.

"I have to make a living as well", she added, a tad defensively, as if that made any difference.

"What," I said, "you have another tenant waiting in the doorway?" She looked down, then dismissed me by turning around. I had been willing to pay more at her place because she could provide human food. I didn't have to eat tasteless base synth like I would elsewhere. But now, I knew it hadn't been worth it. I could have stayed cheaper places, that had no tea and no bread, and now I wish I had.

"I have got a job; I'll get paid soon," I said, "tomorrow for sure."

"Of course, you do," she said calmly, yet her sneer showed me she thought I wouldn't.

"You'll never pay," she said, when I still hadn't moved to

pack my stuff, "your sort never does. You'll just stay on and on and I'll never have my credits."

My sort? What sort was that? An artist? A human being? I didn't know and I wasn't eager to find out.

I had been inside in my studio all day yesterday, working with my last batch, but here on the ground, the gravity was too high, so they grew stunted, and I wouldn't be able to sell them to anyone. The new job wasn't the kind of job one talked about after all. Who would believe real pirates had advertised for a resident artist anyway? They were late, and why would I stay on this ugly moon with its bleak domes, singularly unpleasant population and weird trade that nobody seemed to want to talk about. I mean, who could have guessed?

Everyone else on this moon was from the local system. They were Gobles mostly, and were kinda like humans: Same size as us, different bodies. They had roughly the same nutrient-needs – but very different tastes. No taste buds, I would guess. They lived under roofs, had almost the same kind of housing and air-needs as humans. They often lived on the same planets as humans did. Just not easily. My landlady seemed very friendly with them. I had read about people like her, human-haters who preferred socializing with other species. Why else would she be here? I didn't mind other intelligent beings, but most of the Gobles I had met, were so unartistic and so boring, I preferred my own company. I was fresh out of credits and hence options.

So, what could I do? If I had the stomach for it, I could probably kill her, and take over her house and stay here, of course, but what was the point? Besides, even this lousy corporate mining moon had laws. Yeah, property laws were a big deal, well, property and loitering: staying on after your funds had run out.

They weren't kind to people with no credits. There were no debtors' prisons, but they had *Outside*.

I packed my belongings in a duffel. I even had to carry it myself, as I had to sell my carry-float a week ago. I could grow large plant-sculptures, to refresh the air and hide the ugly dome, but who would pay for it?

So, what did I have? A space-suit of my own. That was pretty cool. It was a high-end suit from my last job. They had it made specially for me, as I was the only human on board. I had some clothes, a formal dress-suit, food for two days in tasteless but nutritionally adequate amounts. A container of water to last as long as the food. My assets were few, my art-education irrelevant. I posted a new application for short term work at the worker's message board and had the board ping me through my internal links if anyone showed an interest. I took a stroll along the inner wall of the dome for a couple of hours, looking at the endless rows of similar factory buildings and houses while I waited for a reply, and ended up right back where I started. No luck. I didn't know exactly when my new employer would be in. The possibility was quite real that they wouldn't come at all. Maybe they had been caught by the authorities.

This was getting scary.

Finally, it hit me. This day might be my final day, ever.

My mind stopped for a moment, and almost closed down completely as I considered being thrown out of the city air-lock and dying slowly of carbon dioxide-poisoning or of exposure. Preferably while being totally smashed on stims, as I had a last stack in my suit for just such an ending. That would be my last such act for the rest of my life, however short that might be.

This was real.

I could do better, but what? I couldn't give up, but

maybe this was how people learned to give up, by not having any options left. The hard way. Well, I was certainly there now and I'd never see my sister again. I took a too deep breath, and coughed. This air was so full of dust. The filters certainly needed cleaning.

Think!

First things first. I needed food and something to drink. Nutrition might help me think better. If I couldn't even help myself, how would I ever get out of here and someday find Elsie? I walked along the streets where the buildings were high enough to almost reach the dome, casting long shadows in the outer areas with poor lighting. Gobles-people were everywhere, but they didn't seem to notice me today. I could disappear in the crowd, but up close, I stood out, being so short, and lacking a few limbs. By a dilapidated warehouse I found a crate and sat down.

I wolfed down a quarter of my last rations.

Wishing things were different. Wishing things had gone better on my last job.

Damn and why did I have to quarrel with that rich idiot? I did actually know better.

Usually.

If this was my last day in life, I would at least take a voluntary moon-walk. Go *Outside*. I had worked on space-ships most of my life, often watched people doing mainte-nance tethered to a ship or fixing struts, dents and commu-nication arrays. I was a fairly good artist after all, and had done sketches and grown sculptures to depict the feeling I got watching them, but I had never walked on the surface of an airless moon.

While I worked here, I never seemed to find the time, and now it was almost too late. I had never been on the outside of a dome. Elsewhere, moon-walks were restricted to wealthy tourists and cost an arm and a leg. There were no tourists here, so why would anyone go *Outside*, pay for additional air, rent a suit and suffer the discomfort of wearing one? Most people didn't have a suit of their own.

Mine was in excellent condition, but I didn't have it anymore. I went by what could only be called a thrift shop, but acted as a pawnbroker as well, but he was a busy being, having lots of stuff to sell. The large humanoid leaned comfortably back on his tail as he watched me talking. He didn't need my services either. I asked to rent my suit for a few hours, but he demanded more credits than I had. Finally, I offered to pay with a food-bar and a quart of water. He accepted; long-lasting protein-rich food, which was valuable for more than one species, was always easy to sell. He said he would let me have the suit for the day, but only if I left another two bars as security.

"Remember, I am closing early today," he advised. "I want to see the new aliens." Aliens? What a quaint concept. A first-contact ship was stopping by the moon for refueling and some minor repairs. Everyone would be there to watch the new arrivals. The guy grinned, his huge incisors newly polished and gleaming. His grin was downright scary. I haggled a bit, and he relented; he would keep my duffel bag with clothes instead of the additional food-bars. I could go without spare clothes, but not without food. The grey jumpsuit I was wearing would be sufficient for most occasions if I survived.

"You can have it until tomorrow," he added. "I don't expect anyone will look for a suit before tomorrow." Or ever, I thought; the plumbing in the suit was species-specific. It would need a lot of work to fit anyone else.

I supposed that he didn't want to come back to the store after the show, just to meet me. We both knew his chance of ever selling it was negligible. Unfortunately for him, food and space-wear were among the mandatory things he had to accept. Even from rare beings such as myself. But then who knew, someone on the next ship might be human. I looked it up on my internal links and blinked away the ads, no, it wasn't a human ship, nor anything I had seen before. Besides, he knew I'd be back. Where else would I find a suit to fit me?

I suspected he did it out of kindness today, at least in part. He still charged me quite enough. The duffel might contain more valuables, at least to him, than the suit. I accepted my suit back and took it to the main maintenance airlock, refilled the stores in it with my water and food-bars, and paid for my required trace-metal-supplements with the tiny rest of my credits. As luck would have it, the CO_2 filters were almost unused. New ones cost far more than I had.

As I donned my good space-suit, the familiar smell of home swamped me, and I felt safer than I had for weeks. Belly not exactly full, but at least not empty, and with my suit on, I felt prepared for anything. Shows how stupid one can be. I felt better, almost human, as it were. I laughed at my own folly and went into the large airlock, big enough for a medium maintenance-vehicle. I donned my helmet, closed the door behind me, and felt momentarily trapped in the small room even before I started the cycle to empty the airlock. Just before the all-clear sounded, the outer door blew, and I was shoved out of it.

Not loudly, there wasn't enough air to carry sound, but forcibly, I and the tiny amount of air that was left, was expelled without warning. My helmet bounced on my shoulders as I landed on my knees on the dusty ground. The inner lock had been sealed, thank the stars, and was still fine it seemed. But I was *Outside*, and this airlock wouldn't work again so I had to find another. The air that followed my expulsion, turned instantly to white glittering snow on my suit. I took one glance around me at the yellowish hills in the distance, and stepped forward in the dust that covered the ground everywhere. As I looked up, I stuck by the beauty of the planet we circled. All of us on this bleak moon. The planet hung large and green in the black sky. To the right, just above the planet, a sun shone far away, giving out enough energy to heat the moon in daytime, but it was far enough away to let us freeze properly at night. The G-type star was much larger than the Earth's sun, someone had said. I wouldn't know, I hadn't even tried to save up for a pilgrimage and had never been on the world where humans originated.

It was daytime, and my suit's batteries soaked up the sunshine. I took a walk, my feet bouncing high with each easy step. It was springy and fun, except landing back down on the ground was quite rough on my knees. The moon was as large as a small planet, but less massive. The artificial gravity inside the dome was supposedly higher than Earth normal, because of the other races, but this felt like a lot less, so I felt lightheaded and started to relax. I knew I should secure my re-entry to the dome, but I couldn't resist exploring. I easily walked up a nearby crater, where I could see the knob on top of the white dome.

The surface was terribly scratched by the winds from the ventilation-systems moving the moon-dust on the inside. It was probably translucent originally, but over time, it had clouded over most places. The outer surface was a different matter. No air and no wind to carry a dust storm; it was a shiny mirror that reflected my space-suited figure. Over the dome, I saw a huge ship preparing for landing in the space-port, the next dome over.

The approaching ship was huge, and strangely shaped. The silvery streamlined shape looked as if it could land in atmosphere. The spaceport dome slowly opened to admit it.

As I watched, the ship suddenly wavered, as if I were watching a bad vid-line, yet not pixelated. Just fuzzy, and for a moment it looked like a giant green soft blob. Then the sleek metallic ship was back. What was this? The ship was let in, then the dome started to close.

The port-dome wasn't pressurized, but the tunnel to the city-dome was. I wasn't close enough to check it myself, but there was certainly something wrong, so I started running, loping towards the port dome. As I came closer, I saw the dome had closed totally, but the blob was real. Something now covered all the ships, and all the pathways, in a dull green sheen. The dome was closed to protect the ships and the infrastructure from meteorites and pirates, but that had not been enough this time. No ship exited, and that was the strangest thing of all. Even if I didn't like the place and tourists avoided it, it was a transit port. The spaceport and the shipyard, both in orbit and on the ground, were usually busy.

There should have been a lot of traffic. I turned my links back on, an eerie silence filled my inner-ear-implants. I had never heard that before. The silence was almost screaming. It was something I had dreamed of, to be able to turn the noise off, the chatter and the ads and the newsflashes. All that was gone. The absence was suddenly nightmarish. I tried all the bands, even the pilot-bands which I was not strictly supposed to have access to. Even that was silent. Something was terribly wrong, and I was *Outside*, not able to see what was happening.

Security used to be good, with two airlocks, and emergency closing of both sides of all tunnels and entrances in case of even the mere suspicion of a dome-breach. Everyone was dependent on it being safe, after all. A few of the airlocks were in the underground tunnels, but most, like the one I had broken on my way out, were above-ground.

I ran over to the main connecting tube. It was transparent, unlike the dome itself. It had a moon view, though partly obscured by hanging plants, like everywhere else accessible. They helped replenish the oxygen. But the walls weren't completely obscured, probably because all people, not only humans, needed to be reminded that they were on an airless moon every now and then.

There were also supposed to be guards.

The large area of green luster I had seen covering the spaceships was here as well. But these were not plants. None of the original plants remained anywhere. Where had they gone? No people were passing even here. It was totally empty and had never looked like this before.

I felt my own heart thumping.

Elevated blood-pressure, said the tinny voice from my suit. *Please calm down. There is nothing to be afraid of.* Was that the understatement of the century!

Sure, there is, I thought. There was everything to be afraid of. No longer afraid of death, I now faced something far scarier.

I had to get back in. Or not. The choice was mine. There were no guards anywhere.

I squinted. Put my face along the surface of the tunnel and glimpsed the inner airlock to the huge dome. It was open. It was never open for more than a minute at a time and it did not close as I was watching. Then I realized that the outer airlock was also open.

They were never open at the same time. It wasn't possible. Not with air and pressure in the dome.

I looked thoroughly into the dome. Then I found the next external airlock, but it wouldn't budge. That was stupid. Malfunction, said the screen next to it. Through my links, I heard the first sound in a while: *The airlock has been disabled for your protection. The interior of this dome is not safe to enter.* Not safe? I had to laugh. Certainly, staying *Outside* wasn't very safe. Not for long.

The dome had several thousand inhabitants and this was the only dome close to the spaceport, the only dome nearby on this forsaken moon. The mines were supposed to be automated, and didn't require domes.

I walked to the next airlock over, a hundred yards further away. The interior here was almost visible, the dome surface less scratched on the inside.

Empty.

No traffic, no people. Just a few abandoned groundcars. That airlock didn't work either. Or the next. This was not looking good. It was becoming harder to breathe, my heart started beating faster, but I had to run, to see if all the locks were ruined. But I knew, even if I didn't want to acknowledge it, I was screwed.

The problem wasn't the airlocks themselves. Yet I had to look. Had to check. I ended up running the whole circumference of the dome, but all were out of order and I had no tools to force them open. And I knew: there was no point anyway.

I was a dead woman.

I recognized the spaceport as I came full circle. I had passed all the other outbuildings around the dome, they were directly accessed, or completely apart, without air. After eight hours of walking and running. I didn't even stop to eat and drink, but had eaten as I walked.

The spaceport, with all the ships that wouldn't let me

get a ride. The spaceport with its roof-top closed again after admitting the alien ship. After opening up to its doom. I had to look closer at what was done to it. There was no airlock from the outside, just an ordinary door. It wasn't even guarded. Then again, who needed a guard there? But what if someone walked, like me, from the dome to the spaceport, wouldn't someone want to know? Well, no one was there to stop me this time.

I had never entered from this side before, from the outside, as it were. I wrestled it open. And of course, there was no air on either side, so it wasn't as hard as expected. I entered the spaceport, a large ceraplastique-covered dome to prevent the moon-dust from entering everywhere. The ever-pervasive fine dust.

The green cover I had seen from a distance was gone. And the ramps and tunnels, tubes from all the ships to the surroundings closed walkways were transparent and empty, bar the odd piece of equipment or two. Some suitcases, travel sacks, bags. All six ships were open. And no one around. Very scary. The base used to be human-owned, before some Gobles bought them out. They liked it there. The only human left had been my, now probably dead, landlady. I am sad to say that I couldn't find it in my heart to feel sorry for her. The Gobles were a greater loss, actually. Were any of them still alive? Maybe some maintenance workers or someone in a suit that were *Outside* when it happened? Not likely at this time, but still. Maybe in one of the other domes, far away, if they were still in use?

I had fourteen hours of air left, if I took it easy. The running had taken more than I had expected. I should have known. Nothing was ever as easy as it seemed. But I was not ready to die yet. Maybe I could access one of the ships on my own? I walked over to the closest and felt like a fly inspecting a house. Standing upright on the ground, it towered over me. Nobody seemed to be around, but I had to get away. There didn't seem to be anybody in any of the ships, either. I pawed the access-plate on the first ship, but it didn't respond. None of the ships looked human-built, most were obviously Goble-built, others: I didn't know. The second ship looked more familiar, possibly originally human-built, but modified. Everything looked to be in order, but nobody here answered my hails either, and I couldn't get in. The silence was unsettling.

Was I alone here?

If so, it had to be connected to the strange ship somehow, but it was nowhere to be seen now. I walked from ship to ship, and tried, but couldn't get in anywhere. I might be able to break in, but that would mean losing my means of getaway. Bad idea. Finally, I managed to work the manual override on the lock of the final ship, and was let in.

My hand-signal was human, an automatic voice said. Whose ship was this anyway? The old woman didn't mention having her own ship, did she? If so, this might be hers. Then it registered, the voice was in elevated Goble-Standard. Oh-ho! A high-ranking Goble-ship. Possibly because I was unarmed, a safety-protocol let me in, and didn't shoot me. I entered, and as I crossed the threshold, the hatch closed, the lights came on and ventilation started to hum. The ship computer proclaimed:

Welcome refugee, it said.

What?

You are the last person left on this moon, and as such, you are permitted to access this ship for a limited time, for a journey to the nearest oxy-breathing inhabited world, within reasonable time.

Was I really safe? The serendipity was too good to

believe. It couldn't be real. Maybe I was dead, because nobody could be that lucky. Least of all me. But here I was, and nobody was attacking me.

If I was the only one left, I didn't have to look around to see if any more people needed rescuing. I could concentrate on myself again. I was here, breathing and safe for the moment.

Please prepare for liftoff, the computer voice continued. I strapped down on a couch and relaxed. The shape of the couch didn't quite fit at first, but slowly the mattress adjusted to my body. The feeling of safety was so unusual, I just fell asleep, or passed out.

When I woke up again, the worry was back. The nearest planet I knew of, was decades away, unless the ship had the new engines. That was not important. The ship was taking me to a planet. A planet with air I could breathe. It didn't matter if I actually needed to go to a civilized planet system. But beggars can't be choosers, and I was just happy to be alive.

But even so, I had to send out a warning to other ships in the vicinity. A message about the green blob masquerading as an ordinary ship, spreading some gas or whatnot that killed all people and all plants so damned quickly. I had to tell about the way it changed its shape to fool the sensors. How it killed everyone and everything organic. The green stuff didn't feel organic, but how would I know? It didn't feel alive. One: It was too quick. Maybe the green blob ship's cloaking device was accidentally similar to the first Gobles ships I had seen? A non-organic goo that ate or dissolved the ship it came in? Unlikely.

But why? Why did they do it?

Was it to kill living beings, was it hungry? Was it to take over the mining-business? Possession being half the battle won. Maybe someone wanted the metals already excavated? What was it anyway? Nanobots? If so, I might have brought them with me.

Oh no. I couldn't do that. Not to anyone. I was in a ship, but where it was going, I had no idea. That was scary enough, and then the warnings from my suit said I was running out of air. I had to somehow make the ship conform to my needs. What kind of atmosphere did the ship's supplies offer? Was the oxygen-mix low enough in CO_2 for me to be able to breathe it? I tried remembering what the air-mix should be for humans, but feared I would have to guess at the exact proportions. The ship informed me that the air was breathable for humans before I even started looking for the proper information. Thank the stars it was interplanetary enough for it to have such a useful database. There was no need to wait, so when the air-flow was stabilized, I opened my helmet and took a breath. Free and stinky air flowed into my nostrils. No coughing, no strangulation. No green goo attacking me. I felt my shoulders relax, I might still survive.

I tried hailing the space authorities in outer orbit, not expecting any answer. All I got was an automatic sequence warning anyone against approach.

Good! The next message was more unexpected:

This port is in lock-down and quarantined due to an unknown pathogen. Landing is forbidden. Ships approaching without proper authorization will be destroyed upon entering orbit.

On entering? What about leaving? I would expect that to be worse if they really feared contamination. Would I be allowed to leave or would they shoot me down? I turned my head and looked out of the viewing port. There I saw the small space station passing by silently.

Nothing happened.

I was so lucky.

Then I was out of the gravity well and in open space on the way to who knew where.

As I unstrapped, the artificial gravity came on, not uncomfortably high. I sat down by the console which actually made sense to me. I struggled to turn off the preordered settings of refugee-ship. I didn't want to go to any Gobles-world. I needed to go to a place with proper gravitational services where I could land a job, so I could save up credits and make myself a new home, not be stuck credit-less on yet another back-water planet.

Or, there was another solution I had to think about.

I rumbled around and the ship provided base synth, just my favorite kind of protein, fat and carb-mix, and nice clean water with no taste whatsoever. I ate, drank water, and slept some more as the ship sailed on into space.

When I woke up again I knew what I wanted. I had a ship and could actually go anywhere I wanted if I could somehow change the destination settings.

It took me several days, but the AI computer eventually let me access everything, after just a tiny bit of haggling. The ship had the fanciest of engines, and guns, and every setting could be altered.

I gave myself a new identity, faked a new ship- ID, and changed the registered owner name to my new chosen self. I was now officially a pirate, and I didn't need to check the laws of any world to know what the punishment for that was: Spacing.

There was no avoiding it if I was caught, so I needed to get far away from here. I just needed to find a way to check if I had brought any bad bugs along first. Where could I go where I didn't care if they all died? A horrible thought.

Nowhere I knew was that corrupt. Except, one place was that bad. The place where this glob of destructive matter came from. I just had to figure out where that was.

So, one more stop before I found my new life and if lucky: New art. I might even find my sister, way out on the frontier.

I had a ship and I had a destination.

THE ULTIMATE THRILL

The posse looked like nothing of the sort, not the expected group of farmers, but people in lace and pure wool coats, not a shred of polyester between them. They were also carefully decked out with pitchforks or sables and large black hats. The poorer ruffians behind them were shouting:

"Off with his head!"

"Off with his head!" They were laughing and brandishing their flaming torches, smoking heavily under the moon in the clear sky. The sky that yesterday had seemed so magical and peaceful, filled with twinkling stars. The constellations in the sky of Sigma III was less attractive tonight. The air was cold, just above freezing.

The throng of people was pushing against him, pulling him almost off his feet, jostling and shoving.

"Help", he heard.

Help, David thought as well, but there is no help to be had.

Not here.

Not now.

This can't be happening, he thought then, running,

panting between the well-dressed louts, scrunched up faces seeping cheerfulness in their violence as he was trying to hide his brand of shame, a glowing flame on his left cheek. I am only a visitor, he thought, a tourist. I haven't done anything wrong. He had thought that with a hat he could pass for a local.

"OFF WITH IT," a man, grinning, stopped right in front of David, pulled up his hand to point at him:

"Here....," the man managed to say, before David's hand punched him right in the face.

Help; thought David again, as he fled further, I am not violent, what is this? But as he ducked under another arm, swinging wildly with a gun in it, a woman beside him turned:

"Here! He's here!" she shrieked, as she discovered him, and David ducked again. Nobody except the closest ones could see him then, but he had to get away from them all. Luckily, he wasn't the only one trying to move, lots of people were trying to get closer to the action, some, one way, some, the other. A light clad fiend stood suddenly before him, and David kicked back, ineffectively against the body behind him trying to grab him, and found a low shrub to grab, and twisted between two others, and ducked under it, as he heard:

"Torch him!" another voice, instigated a chorus of:

"Torch, torch, torch, torch!" It became a steady rhythm; they were stamping like well-trained soldiers, in unison:

"Torch, torch, torch!"

The bush under which he had been, burst into flames, he swirled again, sideways into the other side of the bush; it was slightly quieter there. With his glove, he patted the jacket that was still smoldering. The sodden ground outside the city-walls was deep and his boots kept snagging, he was glad he had taken the time to fasten them properly, even at life peril.

He snuck under another tree that loomed out of evening mist, between the throng of people. Thank God he wasn't the only one in focus tonight. The thought shamed him, to be thankful for others in danger, awful, awful.

The entertainment included sweet girls accused of indecency, three fellows of ungodliness and a frolicking minister. They were all running for their lives. Had they realized the seriousness of the situation yet?

As him, they were dressed in non-flammable wool. Not that it would help, it would just postpone the inevitable. Why take chances, the girls had thought, and dressed themselves as men. Bad choice. It might ease their disguise for a while, but ascertain their eventual discovery. Everything remotely sinful at some point in Earth history, was forbidden here.

"Over here," he shouted into a man's ear, and then ducked behind two other woolen clad men with close shaven faces. The sea of people parted slightly, he had hoped to slouch in between them, but his hat was knocked off his head, and his hair gave him away again. Even in the darkness, fog and mass of people, they noticed.

Why, oh why, had he kept his blond mop of hair, it was too different. Three gleeful women in long dark coats, wool of course, and elaborate hair-do's, grins the size of a monkey's, screamed happily at him, as he had managed to grab his hat onto his head again. Moving, moving, moving away, weaving between them, trying to move partly against the current of people, partly with it. Two shorter women in front of him, in unison shouted:

"Here! One of them, here! Get him!" But they were not looking at David, just having a lark. Fooling the others, working themselves into frenzy. They looked at each other and laughed as others turned and pressed towards them. He sidled away.

Why had he not elected to dye his hair? So proud of his Nordic ancestry, that pride would become his undoing. *Pride goeth before the fall,* he thought, as he moved slowly towards the woods looming out of the mist, hoping against all odds that he might get away.

Then someone shrieked:

"Here is one of them!" Then a woman screamed. What could he do, against all of them? A sea of people was moving like a dark menacing wave towards the sound, a woman in a bright red poly coat rubbed up against him, touching him, grabbing his balls in a decidedly unpleasant and indecent manner. He didn't shout, just slunk down and pushed her away with a sigh. He heard a quirky sound, tweaking wood, and a torch touched the poly, melting it and setting it aflame. With a shriek, she screamed and tried to get the coat off. He watched as it stuck to her arms and burned into the skin. Nobody did anything. Some watched. Some turned towards the next victim. Nobody seemed to care. It made it easier to escape; he just had three more people to pass and the trees could shield him, there were no torches right here. But no such luck, the three moved towards him, and he had to move with them, toward the sound, it would have looked too suspicious if he was visibly moving away from the action. He could hear pounding and more screaming, loud encouragements, and cheering. He came within view of more of the mad people. The stench of fungi-weed was strong on these louts' breaths. The weed was the only acceptable vice.

. . .

THEY WERE on to the women, who were clinging to a tree. Some of the local women were clawing, bashing and kicking at them, and the foreigners were cringing from the blows, begging to be let go:

"Please, please, let us go, we haven't done anything wrong". No, he thought, nothing but being too different, here in the worst place in the system for it. There was no tolerance here. Why did you come here if you didn't look for danger?

"Kill her!"

"Torch her" he heard. As the people around him stretched their necks to watch, he did as well, trying to blend in, trying to stay alive. To no avail. In despair one of the women tried to get the attention away from herself, pointing madly in his direction. He recognized her from the flight here. She was another of the thrill seekers, and had gotten just what she paid for. Just like he had. And like him, he supposed, she fervently wished to be any other place but here. Still somehow waiting for the organizers to pick her up. He hadn't believed they would actually leave them here. Even if he, unlike most of the others, had read the fine print. *If you make it to the pick-up point by midnight, a shuttle will be waiting for exactly one hour*. It said if, not when! No one believed they would not get away. It wasn't that far. But if a rescue would ever come, they would have by now, and he could hear no sign of them.

There was no escape. No way of getting across the woods by midnight. The expensive dream of a special kind of thrill, of outsmarting ignorant frontier-humans had turned into a nightmare.

He tried to creep as low as he could, but the woods were

burning everywhere around him now. His only comfort as he choked on the smoke was that his experience would at least keep others away.

His last message out was: *Sigma III is not a holidaying kind of place. I will certainly not recommend it to my friends.*

The full-sensory simulation was awarded best sim of the week. The next month the public in their ordered life on Earth were queuing up to participate in a life completely off the edge.

THIRST

Heavy-headed Amanda woke up, smelling iron. There were no stars, no streetlights. She couldn't see anything. The ground beneath her was rough and as she coughed and coughed again her throat tore as she tried to swallow the ashy taste it crunched between her teeth. The darkness trapped her.

Gingerly, she placed her hand underneath her and rose up, but dizziness forced her to sit back down again against a hard and uneven surface. She raised her other hand in front of her face, but still she saw nothing. Closing her eyes tightly, red was all she could see. There was no way of telling if she had suddenly gone blind or if it was merely dark. She drew her breath and tasted the air around her: it felt dusty and old, even with an omnipresent cool draft.

Her body was covered with stiff clothes made up of some unfamiliar rough fabric around her hips, narrow and unpleasant. She knew the clothes were hers, just jeans and a shirt. The discrepancy was confusing. She struggled to remember anything, but her head hurt too much, so she stopped.

She tried to rise from the ground where she had lain: Perhaps she was in a mountain cave? What mattered was getting something to drink. She would have to find out what had happened later. Surprisingly, she realized she was not at all desperate. She probably ought to be more worried than she was. She tried again and fumbled to her feet; it felt a bit like a hangover. She remembered nothing; could it have been a party? Why else would she be so thirsty and feel this shitty? Her head pounded painfully as she stumbled and hit a wall in front of her. Reeling back, she hit another wall. On her left-hand side, she encountered a low opening, but feared exploring it. She had never been fond of enclosed spaces and as her pulse quickened, a feeling of dread threatened to overwhelm her. Scared she heard a small whimper from her own lips as she turned around in the silent space. Then, noticing an opening to the right she lurched forward, hoping for a way out of the darkness.

Her hand encountered cool rock. It was uneven and choppy; maybe she was in some kind of cellar? Through her mind ran flashes from movie crime scenes. A little further away her fingers met wood splinters, a beam, rough-hewn and tough. It reminded her of something. This was no basement! It was a mine! She walked on, repeating to herself: This wall was too uneven to be a basement. It had to be a fucking old mine! It was strange, she couldn't remember ever having been anywhere like this. She cocked her head, listening beyond her hurting head for any clue as to where she was. She walked on laboriously, sometimes the rough stone ceiling was so low that it grazed her head, apart from this there was no variety. No sound, no smell, and worst of all, no light. The faint breeze from the direction she headed was all, as it slid against her cheek.

. . .

SHE MUST HAVE BEEN WALKING for hours, with no difference in her surroundings: rock, beam and more rock. She started to feel faint, not surprising, she thought, no food, no water and hung-over probably; naturally she was weak. There was no end in sight, just the same darkness. She approached what felt like a corner, it seemed the mine was turning. She stopped, glided down along the wall to rest. Her ears had acclimatized to the grand silence and she could now discern a weak dripping sound as well as her own pulse pounding in her ears. After a little while it lent her strength enough to get up again and head towards it.

Water, at last! Her stone-dry mouth felt even dryer with the possibility of moisture close by. She needed water and she ran towards the sound. Her nose and hands hit another wall, but the damn wall was dry. There had to be water somewhere further on. She slowed down and let her scraping left hand lead her further along the wall. The horizontal mineshaft had narrowed enough so that she could touch both sides simultaneously. There was still no light, not even at the end. She conceded that there might of course be more bends in the mine, obscuring any potential light. Mines tend to lead somewhere; even a dead end would at least give her a clue to her surroundings.

She wasn't thinking straight, she realized. Like cotton wool: thick fog filled her head, and as she tried shaking it to clear her thoughts a soaring headache resulted. The pain became thundering, making rational thought thoroughly impossible. *No shaking*, she thought and continued to walk along. The headache subsided and thoughts returned slowly. The mine seemed empty, no debris on the floor to stumble upon and no other sounds than those she herself was making as she shuffled along. Moreover, there were no people and no machinery.

If it was an abandoned mine, how did she end up here? She knew that a Norwegian mining town would have been freezing cold at this time of year. At least she thought it was winter, suddenly doubt crept in. She ran her hand over her thin shirt again, noting the absence of a jacket, yet she was not cold. Perhaps a concussion had affected her memory. For all she knew, it could be summer.

The sound of dripping water drew her onwards. Finally, she felt moisture under her fingertips as she scraped along the wall. She quickly put her tongue right against the surface of the rock. Suddenly, intense nausea filled her. There was not enough water for anything other than to make a gluey paste of dust and saliva on her tongue. She tried to spit, but her mouth was too dry. She dried her tongue on her sleeve, not even able to swallow, yet hacked and spit out all she could manage. The nausea subsided, though her temples were pounding again, it was almost as though someone were trying to talk to her in a large crowd, yet she heard nothing.

Her mouth tasted foul, with all the dust, iron and perhaps even sulphur. She walked another few yards and then: Water! A small waterfall from the ceiling enveloped her hands. Flowing ice-cold water slid over her tongue and into her sticky mouth. She filled her mouth and swallowed gulps. Intense nausea returned, and shot through her even stronger than before, and she vomited violently. The liquid tasted like water, yet disgusting, and somehow wrong. Yet she had to have something to drink, she felt she was dying from thirst. She tried the water again, retaining enough of a mouthful to flush out the stone dust and bile in her mouth, but vomited.

Perhaps it was poisonous? She was excruciatingly thirsty; the feeling was overwhelming. How could fluids other than water be running along the wall? Unless it was water that was contaminated. She walked on and on in the pitch-black corridor and a feeling of dread started to fill her. So thirsty! It was definitely worse than before she tried to drink the disgusting stuff. She had to go on, and find a way out in order to stay alive. It was taking too long.

She walked further into the corridor that didn't seem to have an end to it. For a long while she trundled on in the darkness, with a sore hand trailing the rocky wall. The soreness began to bother her, so she switched to the other hand.

Gradually, she started to notice an odor; besides that of rock, and musty wood. It smell was iron-like but the wall was dry again. Abruptly she felt her thoughts beginning to function a little better, but her body was tired and sore after walking so far. She needed to sit down. As she slid down the wall, she tore the back of her T-shirt. Her thoughts returned to ask questions once again:

She had been walking for hours and was tired, but not sleepy, thirsty but not that hungry. She usually had something edible in her pocket, but they were empty. She rested for a moment and then continued. If she were going in the wrong direction, would she even know? Maybe there was an important turn, an exit that she had passed without noticing? Fear knotted her stomach. It was impossible to know which direction was the correct one. The air was quiet now, no more draft. She tried moistening a finger to feel for any draft, but her mouth was too dry. She held her finger up in the air anyway, but felt nothing. Or? Yes, there was a faint draft in the air, originating in front of her, in the direction that she had been walking.

Without thinking about it, she started running, faster and faster towards the fresher air. Step by step she discerned her surroundings; there had to be a light source somewhere ahead. She ran, her feet loud against the ground, a ground that at some point had turned into smooth concrete. A faint light made her finally able to see properly and she shouted with joy, thinking that with light, there would be other people and perhaps even something to drink.

With the growing light came a new smell, weak at first, but definitely becoming stronger. It was in the direction she was running, it was in front of her and she knew she could smell iron. Suddenly she arrived in a corridor; there were proper light-fixtures and hanging pegs on the walls and doors along a smooth wall. She slowed down and walked along the corridor, shouting aloud; nobody answered. It was dead quiet.

She was faced with closed doors and with the force of impatience she pulled them open. The first room was an empty office. Followed by a tiny bathroom. She ripped the door wide open, lowered her head over the sink. She filled her mouth, drank, but then all she had swallowed gushed all over the sink and floor. It quenched nothing. Desperation closed in on her, as well as an increasing sense of anger. She felt her mind turn. Someone had to have done this? How else had she ended up here?

She howled with anger, until her throat became raw and painful, but it didn't help. Someone would pay for putting her in such a situation. She had to get out, and she had to have something to drink, now! Despite her misery and anger she noticed a locked door next to the bathroom. She shook the handle, ripped the door open and stopped.

The light from the corridor revealed a sight she would never come to forget. She walked closer again, and turned on the light-switch to see better. On each and every bed along the walls lay a cadaver. Miners in overalls were all laid out on mattresses; stretched out, as if sleeping. Yet nobody sleeps fully clothed; with their equipment belts around their waists and dusty black boots on their feet.

The stench assaulted her nose, but there was something else as well, a smell of dust. She couldn't stop looking and couldn't stop breathing in the stench - and there was something about the smell that she couldn't place. She noticed their pale faces. It was very, very quiet. No fan to create movement in the air. No footsteps, no noise in the distance, just silence and this smell.

The room reeked of the stench of blood that pushed against her nostrils. Actually, not a stench as such, yes, it was a stench, and then it wasn't. It was disgusting, yet tempting and desirable. She felt an overwhelming sense of need. Strangely enough, she was excited and did not at all fear the same fate occurring to her. She was curious about her emotions. Suddenly, she heard a voice in her mind saying:

Now! Let me have it. I need to drink, or I will die!

Looking at the blood, she didn't believe it. Needing to drink blood was a ridiculous assertion. Then the unbidden voice came:

I must have this blood!

Whose voice was that talking to her in her own mind? Her reason kicked in again:

Where did these ideas come from? She had no idea, but the feeling was intense. Why would she want this? Was she going insane? Desire fuelled her body forward, towards the fresh corpses, but revulsion for herself and for the bodies kept her from going closer. The disgust she felt stopped her.

Her mind felt curiously empty all of a sudden. There was only thirst and the hunger for nourishment. What had she become? This urge was so strong, so overpowering.

How could she resist it and why would she want to? She clung to the doorframe, so it might keep her there, but how long could she resist herself?

The tiny voice inside, echoing bad influence and temptations from her youth, uttered:

You want this, don't you? What's the harm, nobody can see you, and they are obviously dead anyway, they won't mind, they can't feel a thing. Just a little sip to get your strength back, just a lick, and you will feel so much better!

She clapped her hands to her ears, like a child refusing to listen, but the voice was relentless. It was the same kind of insisting, luring voice leading her along a path she was all too familiar with. It was the voice of unreason, the voice of lost friends - of hunger, need and violence. Like the voice that convinced her years ago to try the first E and then...

Her mind shied away from the memory. It was the voice that made stupid decisions seem easy.

"Oh, fuck it," she shouted out loud, "not again" then quieter, she whispered: "I am through with all of that, I am clean and sober. I will not listen to you." The voice in her head laughed mockingly in response. The voice persisted, now with more force, as if fuelled by knowledge of her past weaknesses, by her memories of her wild youth. She stood there, clinging to the doorpost, wanting to run away, yet eager to stay, and to get closer to the -oh so tempting, the -oh so delicious and revoltingly terrible fate awaiting her.

"Fuck no", she repeated, then closed her eyes. Her nose revealed to her all that her eyes were missing. She pinched her nose closed and suddenly, her will power increased. She backed out, turned and fled from the room, down the hallway, further into a new part of the tunnel, hoping to find the way out.

Further and further she ran in the weakly lit corridor,

towards the relief of being anywhere but there. As she ran, she started to see some light, growing stronger as she came closer. She was getting away from the terrible sight, away from the tempting drink and the deliciously awful stench. She ran with her eyes wide-open, thunder in her ears drowning out the tinny voice that urged her to stop and turn back. She ran until she no longer could, and the heaving pained her lungs. She stumbled and fell to her knees, scraping them raw. She got up again and ran on to find a hall with a gate and a closed wire mesh lift.

There was no one here either. Panting and hurting, she leaned against wall by the lift, and sunk down wearily like an empty sack, and fell asleep.

She was awoken by a clanking metallic sound. She jumped, caught her breath before her foggy brain realized she was still in her own personal nightmare. Her thirst had reattached itself to her core.

Thirst! Must have...her mind supplies the word, *blood*. Rejecting it, she repeated to herself, WATER! Water! Water! She needed water. Yet the voice in her head kept insisting:

Blood!!! Warm, life-giving, life-important blood!

"NO," she shouted. She wowed she didn't need anything but water! Even if it would kill her.

She needed anything but blood! But just the thought of blood filled her with a longing unlike anything but sex, and that thought enticed the tinny voice in her mind to say:

Yes, sex and bloo..

No! She insisted. Her scared rational mind cut the thought, but didn't manage to cut the feeling of arousal that accompanied the idea, but instead mentally shunned it away. A clanking reverberated in the hall. A stronger light flooded the room, bringing out sharp shadows and stark edges.

She got to her feet, they were weak and she looked for a place to hide. Suddenly she was afraid, not only of herself, but also for the people coming, who were they? Now she could find out where she was and finally get away from this horrible place. Then the longing filled her, it was a longing for the living, and for fresh flowing blood. This scared her even more now, yet the urges grew stronger, matching the increasing loudness of the sounds.

She crouched behind a metallic cupboard in the corner. As she stroked her hand along its wall, the matte finish rasped her sore fingertips, leaving black residue. Dirty. She would wait for them to either discover her, or for her to attack them. The options fascinated and intrigued her, what might she choose? She didn't know. A thought struck her as she listened to the regular clanking of the elevator descending. What about the six bodies? Where did they come from? What had happened to them?

Then certitude overwhelmed her: She was the only one there alive! Could it be her? Was it possible? Could she have done something so vile and not remember it?

Revulsion filled her, as she, for the first time, had light enough to see the surrounding colors and time enough to look. She risked another peek at her own hands. What she saw scared her more than anything she had ever felt in her whole life. Her hands were not only sticky; her nails were edged in dark brown. She whimpered, knowing she had to get away to hide, even if she remembered nothing of killing anyone. Her reason kicked in again, this was ridiculous, how could she, a small woman, kill six large miners on her own? It was not possible, there had to be another explanation.

Yet she was the only one there; the one alive when they were dead.

What if it was she? She couldn't stop thinking about it, like a tongue on a sore tooth, her thoughts slid around in her mind. What if it really was her? How could she have managed? Six grown men, lay dead in their beds. Why hadn't they woken up and stopped her – or stopped the killer, she corrected herself. If it wasn't her, where was the killer?

She decided to stay hidden, negotiating if she should take the lift up as the men vacated the open carriage. How slowly the lift car descended. It stopped several times on the way down. Now that she was fully awake she realized she should have tried the lift earlier.

The lift was full of noisy talking men; their yellow-helmeted heads were showing through the wire mesh as the lift came within view. She waited and looked at the men, some had large faces and big noses, one had a heavy brow-ridge and a couple seemed tiny in their overalls. She shook her head to clear it. She felt the world closing in on her; the lights from the lift area became a narrow beam of yellow.

She realized that this must be what tunnel vision is like, her head was tingling, maybe she was about to faint? But no, rather another feeling was growing within her; it was rage. With the rage came the thirst and filled her mind. She flexed her shoulders and arms and knotted her hands into fists. She was starting to feel, oh so strong, so deliciously powerful, so sure of herself and sure of what to do. As she felt herself jumping up towards the men, she felt her lips draw back from her teeth in anticipation. A shudder ran through her and she fought for a shred of control one last time; then screamed as loud as her lungs could master:

"RUN, GET OUT!!"

Suddenly she could only see red, could only hear the sound from the thundering rush of blood in her temples. She clenched her jaws together trying to keep control over what her mouth would do as her body was propelled forward into an attack. She tried to regain control of her limbs as they pounded all over the men. She felt her fists connect with some soft body parts, her shins kicked at knees and groins, her elbows pounded into rib cages and her knees into who knew what. Ripping, kicking and hitting soft flesh and hard jaws. She heard nothing, saw nothing, and could control nothing but her own jaw - for now. She was a blind and deaf passenger in her own body. And then, she couldn't feel anything at all.

She woke up, lying beside the lift. Horror surged through her as she remembered the take-over, the loss of control, the desperate clenching of her jaw. Why had she so desperately held on to control of her jaw? She put a sore finger to her mouth, and felt a sticky substance, probably blood. She hoped it was her own, someone might have hit her mouth, but remembering the fight, she doubted that this was the case. Afraid of what she might see she hesitated in opening her eyes. To see the result of what she...no, what her body, controlled by something else, had done. She squinted and saw a frightful heap of quiet limbs. Around her, nobody was awake, possibly not even alive. This should have frightened her, a lot more than it did. Regaining control of her body helped to ease the scare, but for how long? The problem was that she had no idea how she was taken over and let alone how to prevent it from ever happening again.

Evidently, something had happened. The thirst and hunger had disappeared. She was satiated and moreover a contented presence permeated a corner of her mind. The *other* mind in her head, at least this was how she came to think of it.

She got to her feet and looked closer at the bodies around her. Incredibly, not all were dead, as she had feared. Some were only unconscious. Listening, she could hear breathing and she even observed some slight movement here and there. The bodies had torn and bloody necks. She sighed, knowing now why instinct told her to keep her jaws locked, but knew she had to get away from them, or the last one might not live very much longer. She knew the worst now, and there was no going back.

She crept into the lift carriage and carefully closed the wire cage door. The controls seemed easy enough and she pushed a green button to start the lift going up. She gave up the attempts at silence with the noise of the rattling lift. She had control over herself again, though this awareness brought little relief.

She visualized more horror and a terrible future if she couldn't manage to maintain control. Her resolve strengthened. She needed to know more about her internal enemy. But first she needed to get out of here.

Old stories swamped her mind, tales of blood and an image of a vampire scuttled across her mind. She laughed shakily, as if *she* could suddenly turn into a vampire. Her once rational mind rejecting the recent events. If she craved blood, even if she were not a vampire, might she be forced to fear daylight as well? As she neared the end of the ride a light grew stronger over her head. The light was uncomfortable to her night vision and she looked down on her blackened jeans.

That was simply because she spent such a long time in the darkness, she assured herself. She saw no one as she exited the lift at the top. She looked around. Grey corrugated iron over her head told her she was in a warehouse. Narrow wooden beams supported a structure that seemed very flimsy for a mine.

Through a window in the plain grey wall, she saw a pitch-black sky with pinpoints of light, such an incredible number of stars and a clear moon. Underneath the sky was a mass of snow and dark wooden houses with pitched roofs. Behind them were peaked mountains. As she stared out the window, something moved, and she looked up. Green ululating ribbons of light shone in the sky outshining everything. She shuddered as memory came flooding back.

She was on Spitsbergen, the largest island in the Svalbard group, halfway between Norway and the North Pole. It was indeed winter, and therefore dark twenty-four hours a day until the sun would show up and take over in April some time. So, daylight wouldn't be a pressing problem. Missing it however, might be worse, she felt, and suddenly an intense longing for the sun filled her.

With darkness all around, it suddenly felt oppressive without relief. She now knew where she was and she could remember coming here by airplane, hours north of the Norwegian mainland. But how long ago was that? She was incredibly lucky not to have met anybody but the miners. There had to be some police force, even in such a place.

Looking down herself and seeing her shirt and hands, she realized she needed to clean herself up. She had to find a shower, new clothes and get off the island and away. As her eyes became used to the starlight she realized it couldn't be daytime, the few lights she saw from all the houses were too dim.

She found a bathroom and managed to clean up, somewhat. The T-shirt still had stains. She looked around the place, but it was empty and there were no alarms sounding.

Didn't the people of Spitsbergen know what had happened yet? She reached a hallway where she could see a wardrobe and a door. She could turn the knob: It wasn't locked. She slipped outside, drawing her breath with a sharp gust. Her nostrils clung to each other in the biting cold. Her cheeks, surprisingly, did not sting, but her eyes immediately watered in the terrible chill. Her wet T-shirt would surely freeze if she went out. Where could she go? She closed the door quickly and retracted her steps.

Here, at night, everybody was locked inside with solid doors because of the polar bear threat. She had no other clothes, no mittens, no boots, and no jacket or woolly hat. Where were they? She wondered, remembering the warm clothes in her bag when she arrived at the airport. The bag was probably at a hotel, but she couldn't remember which one. She would surely die from exposure! Yet she still wasn't really cold, even after standing in the open door for a few seconds. Now she didn't seem to mind the cold so much. Sighing, she sat down on a bench by the wall.

She had to wait until daytime, even if actual daylight was months away. She needed clothes and there didn't seem to be any in this warehouse-looking entrance to a mine. Surely, someone would come looking for the men down below. Surely, they would come looking for her. She was probably already presumed missing. How did people go missing here, in such a small community? When hiking, or boating perhaps? If she had a snowmobile and a map, or a helicopter, she might get quite far. She laughed, as each option was equally unlikely.

She might go along the coast to the next settlement: the Russian town of Barentsburg, they wouldn't know her there. She could hide there, but these were even smaller villages than the town of Longyearbyen. She felt hopelessness creeping in. She was stuck in the middle of nowhere, in miles and miles of arctic wasteland of ice and snow and the occasional hungry polar bear, within a town of a few hundred souls, who would start looking for the perpetrator, as soon as the next shift arrived to replace the dead crew downstairs.

She had to hide somewhere. Frantic, she started searching the building in earnest. On the walls, there were framed photographs and newspaper clippings of arctic explorers in furs. One woman and the rest were men. All of them were standing beside a stack of furs or next to dog sleds. One stood in front of a ramshackle drift wood hut. This was a strange building: an entrance to a mine that evidently doubled as a small museum.

Her attention wandered at the sight of an empty bottle of Aquavit. Maybe she could drink alcohol, if not water? She felt exhilarated by the idea and continued to search in the wooden old desk and in the ramshackle cupboards. There was even a couch with a blanket, which she grabbed. By the wall was a showcase with old fur clothes, even a large knife: museum pieces. It was easy to break open; her hands broke the frame without her even breaking a sweat. She exchanged her T-shirt for a musty old shirt and a parka. The fur leggings were too long, so she rolled them up, and then added newspaper rolls to the front of the large boots. They were lined with soft straw and covered with fur even under the foot. They were still too large, but she could walk in them. The fur parka had mittens tied to the sleeves and a heavy hood attached. They seemed to be made of seal-fur. The anti-fur activists would shoot her on sight; she chuckled to herself, noting the morbid humor. Though maybe not here in the arctic, she realized. With these clothes, she could go outside. She left the shed and the warehouse, feeling the outdoor chill as pleasant in her new outfit.

In the bleak moonlight, she carefully tried every closed door she saw along the snow-covered road. A movement in the corner of her eye sent her shivering, and as she turned, the Aurora captivated her. So beautiful!

God, how beautiful it was, covering the whole sky. In a huge pinkish star pattern that flew outwards from right overhead towards the mountains in all directions, gradually being replaced by bands of green and yellow snaking behind the mountains. As they started to dim, they revealed an incredible number of stars along with the moon so bright that it hurt her eyes. Then a cloud neared and covered the moon. The aurora waned and darkness enclosed her again.

Suddenly, as she was searching in the sky for more, it returned; the almost transparent, ribbons of green and yellow lights looked like they were being pulled slowly across the sky. She had reached the end of the road and arrived at the harbor. A cruise-ship and a couple of large trawlers were moored just outside the wharf. She could probably take one of the small boats tied to the wharf itself and get out to the closest ship, but first she had to sleep, had to drink and with that thought, a shiver ran down her back. She had to figure out how to deal with her strange mind. She knew she had to stay hidden; at least until her mind cleared.

She walked back the way she came; the harbor held no means of immediate escape. The snow crunched underfoot and it was so cold and hard, it did not even leave a trace as she headed back towards a row of houses. They were all dark.

Suddenly behind her, she heard a siren and she could see lights blooming in the warehouse, and then one by one, in the closer buildings as well. She slipped behind the house quickly. She had to hide and wait. She was grateful for her warm clothes, as she felt unaffected by the cold, she even felt warm. They had to be very good clothes. The old trappers knew how to do things. Unseen, she crouched behind the house, then running from behind the one to the other, ahead of the sounds. Abruptly there were no more houses. Warily she started walking along the road, continually looking back. No one was following her. The road was hard, paved with crusty snow. It was so cold that it wasn't even slippery to walk on; the snow just creaked as she walked along it, away from the harbor, out of town and towards the mountains.

No aircraft fly by night. She couldn't get away to the mainland, away from being caught, but she might get away from the killing and the drinking that she so craved. Maybe the only solution was to leave.

Still satiated and clothed in the old furs, she started walking. It was probably bitterly cold but she still wasn't affected by it, oddly enough. She knew she should stay indoors; it was easy to freeze to death here, she had been told. Lights from behind her swept the road, and she hunched down a bit. A taxi passed her on its way to town. The taxi driver didn't even stop, just drove on in the night. She relaxed.

She should probably cover up, with it being so cold; she could get serious frostbite. Her whole face might freeze, but it didn't seem to matter. Old habits made her cover her face with the collar anyway, but the air she exhaled didn't even show as a warm moist cloud in front of her face. Her breath seemed as cold as the night itself. Her mitten-covered fingers were comfortable. She didn't really know where she was going, she just walked, putting one foot in front of the other, out of town towards the freezing cold and towards the Aurora that was again lighting her way, outshining the moon. The mountain peaks towered over her, with silhouettes drawn sharp with the green light behind them. The lights seemed to sway, not unlike sea grass underwater in slow waves. Ribbons of pink topped the green, and she couldn't get over how strong the light were in the sky, how beautiful everything was - and she was filled with peace. Not exactly hoping to die, just happy to relax as she walked. The crunching of her feet continued as the road ended after a few hours. Only the wilderness remained in front of her now. The hard snow crust held her weight. She experienced a duality of lightness and strength as she walked on and on. Then she heard the voice again: "Where are we going?" She ignored it.

The night seemed unending. She had walked for hours through the darkness being only occasionally interrupted by the light shows of the Aurora. Daytime didn't bring any light. But she didn't care. It was beautiful here, peaceful. Gradually she started to feel the thirst again. Another few hours passed and thirst was becoming more and more of a problem. She persisted. She would not return. Barentsburg would be better, she tried to inform the other mind, trying not to reveal how far that was. The mind in her was weaker now, so she stayed in control. That might be the clue she needed. She could starve that menace right out of her mind.

A chuckle answered her.

Well, if she couldn't escape it, maybe she could use it to her advantage.

For a while she had heard a slight sound coming from her right-hand side. Behind a crest, she noted a padding sound and around the next ridge a large shape moved against the snow. She saw the frosty smoke of breath.

A large yellow-white beast started loping towards her. At first it resembled a furry dog, on all fours. Growing nearer, its teeth shone coldly white in the starlight. She had no gun, just the knife in her belt, which suddenly seemed so puny, even if it reached her mid-thigh. Curious and coldly interested she noted that her pulse was slow as she stared into the polar bear's black eyes. She should be afraid but she wasn't.

Slowly she drew the knife from its sheath and felt in her mind for the rage that took her over last time danger was close.

Are you there? A chuckling voice answered the query.

So, you welcome me now, do you? But of course, this time we can do this together. She shivered, anticipating the attack.

The fresh blood will do us good, won't it? Even if it is from a beast. A vague feeling of regret slipped past from the other mind in her brain, but she didn't know if it was regret for the beast, regret for itself or for her. Not that it mattered right now.

She felt the bloodlust gradually take hold, but this time she didn't fight it. This time she was present, aware of it and willingly participating. She pulled off her large mittens, grabbed the knife in her bare hand and attacked. Her knife tore and cut into the loose fur covering the beast's neck. She clung to the large animal as it raging tried to rip her apart with its pointed claws and long canines.

Bite it! the voice urged.

She cut and bit into the neck before she was ripped up and fell off the animal.

She looked at her own new wounds and felt them open as she took hold of the bear again, but her body was so weak. As the bear attacked, she put her mouth to the bears neck-wound and drank from the flowing well of red, the drops freezing to ice rubies in the fur. She drank and swallowed before tiredness filled her and her body relaxed. The voice was faint now as it said: *Goodbye little one, we'll both be gone soon A bear has such a powerful spirit, there won't be room in its mind for either of us.*

She lay quietly watching the snow as it drifted slowly from the sky to cover her. She slept.

As she woke again, the world was fresh. She relieved herself and scratched behind her ear. Complacently she nudged the small body next to her, stiff, yet strangely familiar. She was thirsty, so munching the carcass looked tempting. Taking a bite of the frozen meat was no problem. However, it didn't taste right so she vomited promptly. It did not worry her at all. Her snout itched - so she rubbed it in the snow to clear it.

She whined a little, she was starving and knew she needed to find food soon. She could smell the sea. The back of her front paw brushed some of the frozen blood from her snout, and she licked at it. Delicious. Human blood kind of delicious. Then she picked herself up, and started walking.

Her limbs felt odd, so she stood up on her hind legs, managing to walk that way for a short while, but tired of it and dropped down on all fours, and continued her normal gait. Her mind was filled with the image of snow and ice, looking for a reindeer or a seal; there might be some around, even if the sea was far away. She couldn't smell any humans nearby. Then, she remembered they were down by the sea. She longed for the sea, to swim so freely and everything was perfect for hunting. She strode along the valley, towards the shore and towards people with blood in them.

Tasty!

As night fell, she felt it in her bones. She dug a shallow cove into the side of the hill and lay down in it to sleep.

The next morning, she continued to walk on, towards the smell of the sea in the air. There would be food there: humans, seal and fish and the occasional walrus, filled with the red flowing drink that she so craved.

THE ORPHAN AND THE TROLL

The silence was overwhelming. Cecilia swiped the screen away and cut the power, having finally made up her mind. She would walk through that port one last time and tell another story, a real one this time.

She put on her suit to protect her from the colder air, but left her helmet off as usual, before she stepped into the airlock. She left the gun unpowered in the drawer by the door. As she opened the outer door, the familiar screeching tore at her ears, but she managed to ignore everything until her new earpieces could adapt to the thinner air, and her lungs to the stinky atmosphere. She took a careful breath and nausea gripped her, but only for a moment. She was getting used to it all. The smell was sickly sweet and something she used to know, she thought the first day.

She had run a smell-comparison, and gangrene was what the screen pronounced. Of course: that same smell had come from her grandfather's arm just before they cut it off, way too late of course, before she was moved to the orphanage, before she went to space.

At first, she had to crouch to go through every doorway

in the ship. This stupid ship was so small. Why build it so small, why was the ceiling so low, she had complained to the vice-captain, her confidante, the one who had rescued her from her home-town as he passed through. He had asked for volunteers to yet another one-way mission to the stars. To a no-name planet around Beta this time, since they hadn't heard much from the previous ones. But she was fed up with her orphan school life, and her foster-siblings, even if they were a nice bunch. Her foster-mother was a very nice person, and had taken care of her and her foster-siblings all her life.

But dull.

She couldn't talk to any of them about anything but everyday life. Well enough, but life was more than that, wasn't it? They were all just occupied with small frugal goals, one should never want too much; never aim too high, was the message she got whenever she dared voice her long-ings. They always harped on how grateful she should be – and she was. Very. She owed her life and her education to these strangers in a foreign country, but when the vice-captain came by on his visit before he started intensive training to go on such a long trip and needed volunteers to go with him? She hadn't hesitated even a minute. It was a dream come true, totally fantastic to be able to travel, to get away and to go where no orphan had gone before. She couldn't wait.

And here she was. Without any of them, and she missed them so much.

Suddenly the noise became intelligible sounds, as she tilted around the corner, and her body sagged as she strug-gled to adapt to the heavier artificial gravity there. A deep breath, and physically it was no worse than getting out of a pool after an exhausting swim.

She leaned carefully sideways to enter the large and rather empty room beyond to meet her recent acquaintance. A few more deep breaths and she could largely ignore the smell.

"What have you got for me today?" Troll asked, their bulbous face staring at her, stalked eyelets protruding in a cluster from the large brownish mass of their body. They, he or her? She had no idea if they even had genders. There were no recognizable signifiers, yet strangely enough it seemed relevant, as if alien personhood needed to be gendered, like old timers. She knew it didn't, so shook her head at her own hang-ups.

"You said you'd tell me another story!" they said, and the stink intensified. Yes, she thought, I did promise to tell them something. Naturally you want to know where we came from, how we got to be here, who we are and if my species are more dangerous than I am.

"We..." she began, "the others, we are all different. We used to be a single-star species." She hesitated. "Some of us love exploration, others not."

Yesterday she hadn't been able to go on at all, just fumbled. And Troll had let her do so without interruption. She had to focus. This friendly being did not want to know that humans kill each other, and she didn't want them to know that her race tended to expand everywhere possible, that humans had emptied and polluted even their birth planet. She did not want to tell them that history.

Then again, why not? Why did she cringe from disappointing this being? But what could she do? Would she lie? No. That was out of the question, this was a first contact after all.

"I do have a story for you," she said. "But this time I want a story in return." Eagerly she awaited their answer.

Would they play along? She had been here for weeks now, and counting. The problem was that she no longer knew where in space she was. Her ship's course had changed several times. So, by now she could be anywhere between Earth and the Beta colonies. Even that was not certain, she could have doubled back without noticing – or could have overshot Beta-planet completely, by way of the star that was suddenly in her path. Which idiot had entered the course that would put the ship in the vicinity of this neutrino star anyway? The power-boost needed to get her out of its path threw her off her original course, naturally.

Later she would have to compute another vector change because of being pulled into the hold of the alien's ship. She was forced to follow its path for a time, but had no knowledge of how fast they were going, or which vector they were cruising along. If the ship computers hadn't traced every change, it was hopeless. She was certainly off track because Troll's ship was a totally unknown factor, something which would have disrupted the instrument readings ever so slightly.

She knew it; she would never see the promised world Beta-four, the fourth planet around the second closest star to Earth. There was no point in trying; she didn't really know how to plot the new course. She'd had no formal astrogator training, just learned by watching. Which, when you came right down to it was really stupid. Everyone should know how to navigate between the stars. If she came through this alive, she would certainly learn it.

She was still alive, that was an unexpected bonus. There was enough recycled water to keep her drinking for a long time. For now, the hydroponic vegetables and runner beans gave her sufficient food. But enough protein would be a problem soon, if she lived long enough to miss it.

What kind of an alien was Troll, as she had named them in her mind? They hadn't offered her any name. If she managed to communicate her needs more precisely, Troll might be able – and willing to rescue her from starvation someday. She smiled at the idea of getting them to give her food again, hopefully something digestible this time, and preferably tastier-looking than last time. But that had to be a problem for another day. She had enough on her mind today.

After the usual session with Troll, she was exhausted. She ate her supper, drank enough of the vanished captain's wine to knock her out, and slept for hours. Afterwards she watched a movie and wrote an account of what had happened, before she showered, dressed and knocked to be let into the airlock again. She couldn't leave the area, but she couldn't stay away from the alien ship either. The sessions with Troll was the only thing keeping her from dying of boredom.

She had stalled at first, after its barrage of questions:

"What exactly do you want to know? There is not much I can tell you, I know only what I have seen." She could opt out that way, she could tell of the world she knew by direct experience, and skip the history-lesson, skip the war-stories from Sierra Leone her mother had told her about, skip Afghanistan after the Americans left, and her South African great-grandfather's survival despite the loss of both his arms.

Skip the latest news from Earth.

Skip the world wars.

She hadn't experienced any of it herself, after all. The stories she grew up with might not even be true, but she knew they were. Why would people leave if they could stay at home?

"I want to know everything about you," Troll said.

"And I want to know everything about you," she responded. Did she notice a hesitation just then? And what if she did, would it mean the same as with humans? She had no baseline, and no fact to corroborate it. Why should Troll react as a human would? They were very far from human-looking. Except, she thought, she did have some real experience: The creature had already reacted surprisingly similarly to what a human would in similar conditions. Then she laughed to herself: No, they hadn't, she had to admit, they had behaved as she would have wished a decent human being would do, on a particularly good day. Meaning it had not hurt her in any way, which a lot of humans would, she had to remember. She could afford to guess how Troll's reactions were relevant. Suddenly she noticed something else, as she was studying their face more thoroughly. They were listening to someone, every time they hesitated – that made sense. How weird was it that she hadn't noticed before?

"Are you communicating with someone else than me right now?" she asked and couldn't stop herself from laughing. The look on their face was ridiculous. Sheepish would be her guess, if they had been human. They hesitated again, more noticeable this time. Then they actually answered her properly for the first time.

"Yes!"

Finally, she was getting somewhere.

She wouldn't have shown the holos, just still pictures, nor the frantic voices recounting bits of yet another catastrophe, as her skip was hurtling further and further away towards the new colony so very far away. She couldn't get there on her own without damaging her own ship in the process. And she couldn't get help, because she had no way to find the way back home. But now she was here, supposedly telling a story, but the real story was the one about what had happened to Earths humanity. She was not ready to tell that story.

When she awoke from stasis, she was alone in a tiny escape pod. She had searched nearby for her ship, and surprisingly she found it right away, it was not even far away. The ship was in orbit around a dead moon, quite empty, with all the escape pods ejected, and most of the supplies gone. There was no message, no recording, and no explanation of any kind. Yet everything was working, as it should. What had happened to the others, her adopted family, her so-called friends, and her real friend shipmates?

It was strangely quiet with so many people gone. The ship had been built for a large crew being there for a short time, but mostly a skeleton crew for months or years if need be. Stasis kept the rest in safety. Though this long exposure to the stasis-field's side effects were unknown. The Betas knew of course, as they had been through it, but that information had been sorely lacking in the reports sent back.

As she entered the huge colony ship the first time upon being released from stasis, she discovered that the crew was not the only thing missing. Hundreds of sleeping colonists were gone as well. She was too far away from Earth to turn back when she awoke, and now, the alien ship was there, right beside her ship. Troll and their companions could have been the ones who moved or killed everybody, or they could be innocent. They were certainly curious. Just happened to come by? Not very likely! Yet she didn't actually know for certain, and it was a first contact. So, she had to act as if they were responsible, without antagonizing them. Yet gain their help in some way? An impossible task.

They seemed eager to understand, to communicate, but

only for short periods of time. They quickly learned the words she used – but no other words. They did not try to teach her anything of their own language. Why was that?

Very unusual – again, unusual for a human. She had to stop thinking of them as human just because they were intelligent.

"Where are you from?" she asked as her routine first question, like every other day. Then:

"Where are you from?" a perfect pronunciation in her own voice. Creepy! Startled, she had reacted to that. Then realized, it had to be a recorder. But were they parroting, or were they trying to learn her language? The next answer they gave sounded differently. It was in a different pitch and speed, and not like her voice anymore.

"I am here," their response had been.

"What are you going to do to me? Where are you from?" She had asked. But they had not responded to that. After a while of waiting, she had left and gone back to her quarters. They never tried to follow, and she never had to use her gun. She returned after eating.

"Hi again," she said.

"Hi again," they answered.

"Have you been here long?" she said. It was a first contact - she should be elated. But her situation: alone, dependent and imprisoned as she was, made her less aware than she probably should be. She recorded everything, just in case someone might one day read her story. She almost laughed by the mere thought. Wishful thinking. She refocused to concentrate on the conversation right there:

"Yes," they said.

"How long?"

"A very long time?"

"What are you doing here?"

"To consider. Watching you."

"Me?"

"Yes."

"Do your people live on many planets?"

"Yes."

"Is it far from here?"

"Yes."

"Have you ever seen any others looking like me?"

"No, similar, but not like you," they answered.

She had tried to ask more specific questions, but got no better answers. They just gave vague, uninformative answers, and only in words she herself had already used. Just like the ones she was giving out herself. She couldn't think they were scared of her, one human alone in space, with a ship ten times as big as hers, containing who knows how many beings, and how many weapons.

Every day they were there, waiting on the other side of the airlock. When she had first spotted the vessel, panic tried to take control. Then thankfully her training kicked in. She had to hide the most important stuff, in case they managed to read her files. She scrubbed the computers of all human history, as well as maps showing Earth and the Beta colonies. Everything had already been made ready for it, in case of capture. It was done as a bit of a joke, as no one had ever seen signs of animal life outside of Earth before. There were barely native plants on the Beta planets, and even less elsewhere. Still the protocols had been set up for just a situation. Scary to think about, but she couldn't override the actions; her training was too unambiguous, the warning too strong.

"If I tell a story," she continued, "you must tell me one in return." Again, she noticed that faint hesitation. Then:

"Yes," they said. "A story."

Today was the real test of what was in store for her. She would test the alien being's views on killing. The last time she tried, they hadn't answered.

She had brought a chair and a replika of an old paper book called: *Fairy tales*. A relic from her Nordic ancestors, a children's collection of Asbjørnsen & Moe's fairytales. They were stories of poor, but cunning people, evil kings and huge stupid monsters. It was quite fitting; the being resembled a troll, only smaller. She had snickered as she read through her favorite story, and prepared to tell the tale. Troll squatted next to her on the bulkhead, while she was holding on to the tiny chair as the ship moved under them.

"What is happening?" she asked. The ship was definitely turning, accelerating. She stood up, book in hand and looked at her own screens. She might not know exactly where she was, but her instruments had kept track of the distance travelled since she reset everything. The ship was moving towards the area she had been picked up.

"Where are the rest of my crew?" she asked.

"Safe," they said.

"Where are they safe?" She couldn't stop herself: "In what way?"

"I don't know."

"Can I see them?"

"No."

"Why not?"

"Not safe."

Frustrated, she wanted to scream. But instead, she sat down and tried to interpret what this Troll was doing. Analyze it, as a rational human being, even in the face of danger. That was her one strong point, wasn't it?

One: They were interviewing her, definitely. Actually, it seemed more like a debriefing. They were recording.

Were they some kind of lawyer? No, they never contradicted her descriptions, and only repeated a question she hadn't answered. They didn't try to lead her in any direction, so not a military creature, and she never saw a weapon. That could have other reasons; it could be unrecognizable, or just hidden.

"Tell me," they said.

"What? Where are we going?" she said.

"We are taking you home," they said. Her heart started to pound, and she shuddered.

"That is nice," she managed. "I don't know how to find my way there, do you know where it is?"

"We know, they said, "now tell me the story."

So, she did.

Once upon a time, there was a boy living with his mother and father. They were very poor, and told him to go into the woods to find kindling and wood for the fire, since the winter was cold that year. The white frozen snow was waist deep, but his skis were home-made and sturdy, letting him slide on top of it.

"What is snow?" Troll asked.

She snickered.

"Snow is frozen, crystallized water. Made up of two hydrogen atoms and an oxygen atom. It is what I drink when I am thirsty." The being stood up, transfixed, staring at her, listening as she continued. Probably recording everything, even if she had seen no devices before. They had one now. A little round mechanical box was visible on Troll's thick neck. They asked no more questions. She continued:

As the boy came into the woods, he met a troll. He scurried under a nearby fir-tree with low hanging branches, and removed his skis to hide even closer to the stem.

The troll was gigantic, towering over him and all the

dense green trees. It couldn't see him, but sniffed around in the woods with its three heads, the one uglier than the other, looking for the boy who was cowering under the tree, trying not to be noticed.

That got the attention from the huge being opposite her:

"Was the boy afraid?"

"Yes, she said, very!"

"Why? What is a troll?" said Troll.

"A large being," she said, "they are very scary."

"Why are they scary?"

"They are terribly dangerous." It was hard not to smile, could she just pretend? Would she get away with it? Then she relaxed and smiled to herself. Why not?

"How big are they?" they asked.

"How big trolls are?" She laughed, shakily, and said truthfully: "Trolls?....I have never seen one myself, but they say the smallest are five times my size, and the biggest are huge as mountains. As a child, I was scared stiff in the evenings whenever I heard any kind of sounds from the woods."

"How many trolls are there on your world?"

She smiled, this was too entertaining for her not to continue, and she felt like a proper storyteller.

"I don't know, mostly they seem to ignore humans, when they are not eating them," she added, feeling that might be true, if trolls had ever existed for real. Troll stood up, righted themselves. Glared at her for a moment.

"How do you fight them?" they asked, as if curious, as if falling out of their usual passive interrogating role. Did she want to explain? Did she want to play with that idea? It was, after all only a fairytale, so she continued.

"With sunshine... they can't live when the star on our planet is shining."

She took a sip of water from her helmet, swallowed and closed her eyes. Strange, she thought. Thinking it felt too real, she could almost see a huge a Troll standing in front of her, and suddenly the water caught in her throat. The image was suddenly as terrifying as it was when she was a kid and she hiccuped.

"You are scared," they said in a changed, lower, kind of soothing voice. "I am sorry."

"Yes," she said, "they are very frightening." Troll looked at her, grey slender eyelets staring into her eyes. As if ...? No, she didn't know. But there was something there, something she should understand, but didn't.

"Do they travel in space?" they asked.

She giggled.

"Not yet. They prefer the mountains and the woodlands to open space."

"Please continue," they said.

She waited, while halfway musing over what role Troll had. Were they alone? Then she continued the story:

A large hand came trashing through the branches and grabbed the boy, he was suddenly lifted into the air and held before the middle head of the Troll.

I want to eat him, the left head, said.

I found him first, the middle head said. No, you didn't, the right head said, besides, I am the hungriest, so I should have him. The boy shook and shivered.

Help, he said. But none of the tree heads bothered to listen. It was no use, no one would come and help him, he was all-alone. But the boy was clever. He thought that if he could get them to quarrel about who would be eating him, he might get them to fight as well, and anything that could postpone the inevitable dividing up and eating him was a good thing.

Hey, he shouted at them, and kicked the thumb of the hand that was clutching him. The hand shook him as response. Which of the tree heads were controlling the hand, he wondered, was it the middle head?

Hey, he shouted, even louder, you - the middle one!

What? it said, irritated, and did not seem to appreciate the food talking back at it, but without shaking him this time. Maybe it wasn't in control as he had thought. Then he said to the middle head:

You certainly can't have me!

And why is that? it said menacingly. The boy looked at the other two heads, first the left head, then the right one. They gazed right back, and then nodded.

I am too good for you alone, I belong to the smartest of the three of you, he said loudly. The large floppy ears they had on each side of their bald heads seemed to work quite well.

What? The middle troll-head, said. The one to the left, said: Yes, that's right, because the smartest one is me! The right head scowled at the other two, and said, -no waay! You two wouldn't know how to do anything if it wasn't for me.

Troll sat very still beside her, their lumpy body warm to the touch, not fuzzy, but comfortably smooth. When had they moved this close? She hadn't noticed them moving as she was talking. Then they moved away a bit and turned, looking at her again, eyestalks swiveling towards her and away.

"Could you show me an image of the troll?" it asked. She pulled out her precious memento of her great-grandmother. She who took care of them all and bullied the whole family to move towards safety, again and again as the war came closer and closer.

Troll studied the ink-drawings, most of the eyestalks pointing at different parts of the book, while a few remained on her. Looking at the script and at the black-and white etchings.

"Only flat?" they said after a while. "Don't you have anything more realistic?"

"No, sorry. That is all I have, an artists' representation."

"Do you not have a database of some kind showing creatures from your planet?"

"No, I don't."

"Why not?"

"Why would I need one? We didn't expect to meet anyone out here," she countered.

A pause, then they said:

"It looks a bit like me. Maybe we are distantly related."

"I don't think so," she said. "We live far from here."

"So do we," they said.

After a few days of not very good communication, Troll met her at the airlock and held out a small lump of dough.

"What is it?" she asked.

It pointed at her head: "To speak my language," it said. "Good for ear."

She looked at the pink goo. "Shall I put it in my ear, or what?" She pointed at her left ear.

"Yes," they said. She put it in her bad left ear and waited a bit. Now what. Loud screeching started and abruptly she heard in her left ear:

"Wait for translation," in understandable One-speak English and: "How does that feel?"

"Good," she had to admit, but as she heard the screeching at the same time, she held one hand over each ear and asked: "Do you have one for my other ear as well?"

"Of course, you have two, yes," then they disappeared.

The goo transformed itself in her ear, hardened and did some fancy work, so even the loudness was better.

Soon after, Troll returned, and gave her a second putty, which she promptly put in her other ear, and they could speak for real.

"Who made your spaceship?" Troll asked.

"Some people, I don't know," she said.

"Trolls," they asked?

"No, certainly not. Other of my kind did it."

They didn't try to teach her anything – so they were no teacher. At least not one she could recognize. All this of course, assuming human logic could be applied. On the other hand, she had no other information. She was a rational being herself.

If you don't have any data to support an opposing theory, you keep your original theory, don't you? Continue with the information gathering. Surely it was better to be doing something, than just giving up. She wasn't ready to give up yet – no way. She felt better and she chuckled. The large cabbage-leaf ears turned limberly towards the sound.

"You are amused? That is good."

"Yes."

Troll seemed to react as if she were a skittish mouse. They let her have an option to flee whenever she wanted to. They never stayed very long. Ah. Now she noticed. The amount of time they spent together was increasing. Their vocabulary was increasing tremendously. They were a very friendly being who seemed to react as a friendly human would towards a frightened animal. But they didn't let her see any of her family or shipmates, which actually was a relief. They kept her isolated from her fellow humans, but also from their fellow Troll-beings – if there were others, and she could safely assume, because of the ship-size alone, that there may very well be lots of other aliens.

Ha, she thought: She was the alien! They, on the other

hand, might even be at home here. She herself was the scary being from outer space! If she were the alien, what could that mean?

Was she in some sort of quarantine? No, that wasn't likely, as she could move freely about, and breathed the same air as Troll, and they were allowed to even touch her.

Was Troll a kind of risk-seeking doctor? No, they hadn't examined her, had taken no test-samples like blood or anything, and didn't seem interested in her physical wellbeing, apart from regular needs, like thirst and hunger.

Could Troll be a shrink? They didn't feel like one, and didn't seem interested in her mental wellbeing. Fright – that seemed to gain their attention, and definitely anger! They were also deterring her from what she wanted to do, with their long conversations; maybe they were stalling her in some way?

A human in Troll's position? What purpose, what set of options would make sense out of their actions? She scoured her memory for clues. She had been here months now. Were they moving again? She hadn't checked the instruments since the last movement. They seemed to try and keep her from danger and seemed to want to pacify and occupy her. Had they fed her at any time? Sort of.

Well, perhaps. The first time they met, they had given her a brown sticky-looking lump of matter in an open box, and a plastic vial of muddy vile-looking liquid. But she had been overwhelmed and scared enough to reject anything they offered. She didn't know whether it was water or protein she could digest or any other useful information. They hadn't offered her any food or drink again. She might have to ask it for a test-sample soon, and shivered by the thought. With no samples of her, as far as she knew, how could they decide if she could eat something? Maybe they were more advanced than she knew, and just a stray hair would be enough of a sample to know what she needed? Maybe.

Now the box was back. Troll handed it to her:

"What is it?" she asked.

"Eat," they said. "Food and drink for you."

She lifted the box up and tried to leave with it. Troll said: "No! Stay here." She complied, scared. What had just happened?

"Not box," it said. She lowered the box, but kept the vial.

"No," it repeated. Then she put down the vial as well. They said nothing. She was not allowed to bring it into her own quarters to test it for edibility. So, she didn't dare try to eat it.

"I will bring food."

She still had her own food, and went back and brought some and handed over to Troll with a glass from the last wine bottle. She took a bite of reconstituted meat and potato and lifted her wine glass, to show how she drank it.

They reacted strangely to the wine, tried to stop her. She left the glass and the food on the table, and they did not follow.

When she came back, the table had a plate of spinach-like green goo on it. The liquid in the glass was clear.

She tried a small bite, and it was strange, but she did not vomit or die, so she took another bite. The drink was water, pure, distilled water. She thanked them, very relieved. After a bit of prompting, she went back to telling the rest of the story:

The three heads only shared two arms, so the boy lured the troll to let him down so they could fight each other properly, and they did. In the end, the troll knocked itself out and stumbled to the ground where it fell and slept until sunrise. As the first rays touched its skin, it cracked loudly and turned into stone.

She looked at Troll and said:

The place is still called troll meadow because of the crumbled remains of troll rock.

Troll gave her more food and she kept telling stories, all the stories she had ever heard. She recounted every book she could remember and summarized every film she had ever seen. Still they seemed eager for more.

There was a story of a man who was hungry all the time, and he walked around in a city somewhere searching for work and food. There were a lot of descriptions of his hallucinations and of how he treated people badly because he wanted to appear to be rich and clever. Instead he put people off, even the ones who liked him or felt sorry for him. He fell in love with a pretty woman but she scorned his lack of manners and coarse speech. Or was that it? Anyway, he thought she hated him because he was poor.

Stupid man, she thought. Cecilia couldn't quite remember how it ended, so she made up the rest, and she was certain it was very different from the original. Not that it mattered, because Troll listened fascinated, ear holes glistening.

The days passed, with little change. One day she asked to explore Troll's ship, but they said no. Then one day she felt a shudder in the ship. She had been relaxing in the media-room, drinking hot tea and eating bean stew with the last chili in it. A klaxon sounded, and she let the rest of the food on the table, ran to her quarters and rapidly put on her suit. She even donned the helmet this time, before she ran towards the air lock. The speakers in her helmet boomed and screeched, and she had to remove it again to be able to hear what Troll was saying.

"Please come over. We are leaving," they said.

Leaving? What would happen to her? the Betas, and to the Earth? What had she been doing, not thinking clearly, that's what, she said to herself. She should have discovered more about the alien, and she should have saved herself, gotten away from here, she should have been looking for her family and the crew-members.

"I want you to meet someone," Troll said as she arrived in the opening. She looked around the corner: For the first time, there was someone else there in the room. A being much like Troll, only greener and so huge. And lumpier, and flabbier somehow. Awestruck, she couldn't speak at first. Then they said: "Greetings!" which made her giggle, and furious at herself, she swallowed the mirth and said:

"Greetings to you too!" Who was this person, what did they want? Strange. It was so formal compared to Troll, whom she was getting quite familiar with.

The nauseating smell of corruption, rot and decay.

"Are you well?"

"Yes, I think so."

"Is something wrong?"

"Just the smell.

"Does the smell bother you," they asked.

"Yes," she had to admit, as they seemed to be able to change it and to such a degree was amazing. "It is uncomfortable."

"Do you want me to change it?" they asked.

"Please, yes!"

"I will do it before we meet again," they said.

The next day, the smell was different. Still she became nauseous, but it was not quite as revolting. A milder version, like faint vomit and poo mixed, but infinitely better than before.

"Can you tell us more stories?"

"Yes, I suppose," she said.

"Do you need to live on a planet?"

"Probably. But not necessarily, as long as I can move around a bit," she added. "Why? Where are we going? Where are you taking me?" She started to feel queasy.

"Could you live in space?" A bit frightened, she said snippily:

"Not without atmosphere, I couldn't."

Troll interjected: "We mean on a space-station. The larger being ignored the lesser.

"We want you to tell stories there," they said.

"Me? Like I have been doing to you? Hm. Oh, that is possible, I suppose. But a space station sounds like a very cramped area for permanent habitation. Where is it?"

"It is a very big space station." Thank god. Something the trolls called big would surely be large enough for her.

"Then perhaps I could live there for a while." Curiosity propelled her to say:

"To whom would I tell stories? I have told you so many." She thought it wouldn't be a good idea to tell them that she had told them nearly all she knew.

"To our young ones," they said. This was a new turn.

"Oh." She was dumb-struck. She, a storyteller or teacher? What an idea! Well. Maybe she could do that? Furiously, she thought through it. What else could she do? A job sounded like a good thing. She might even be paid.

"Yes," she said. "I would like that. But I cannot accept such a gracious offer without knowing more about you and about what has happened to my crew."

They looked at each other, the bigger and the smaller. And she noticed a weird wobble in the larger one.

"They have been transported to their destination without their ship. Unfortunately, we destroyed the engines, we thought they were weapons, you see."

She had been in quarantine, and while they waited, they talked to her, learning as much as possible about this slip of a thing, surprisingly enough an intelligent being, Troll said. And that was a funny prospect; when she found out, she smiled, as she had always considered herself quite large and very ungainly on Earth because of her height. She was so tall that she often had to crouch as she walked around in her own ship, but not in the alien ship.

"Have you really transported my crew to...?"

"Yes, we have".

"Why?" She was skeptical.

Then they showed her a holo-film of the large Beta-sign of a planet-colony and among those who stood to the front, was her vice-captain and the rest of the crew. Behind them milled a large crowd of what she imagined had to be the colonists.

Relief filled her. She didn't have to feel responsible for them anymore. Then it struck her, she should have been among them, yet was relieved that she wasn't.

"Why did you do that?"

"They would have been in danger."

"From what?"

"Us. We are not ready to let large amounts of a new species into our home-space without knowing more about them."

That made sense, she supposed.

"How did you transport them, when the ship is here with me?"

"They were already in small escape vessels. Maybe they were scared. We just rounded them up and left them at the closest inhabited planet with the right atmosphere."

"Fantastic! But why didn't you bring me as well? Why did you keep me here?" She couldn't decide if she was anxious or exited. "Does that mean I don't have to go there?"

"Not yet. When you have trained ours, we will go together. Stories unites us as imaginative beings."

Troll looked at her and asked anxiously:

"Would you prefer to go with them?"

"Probably, eventually," she said. "But not yet. I want to tell stories first, and meet your young ones."

"Then you will!" The large Troll said. "Troll here will show you what you need to do, and show you around. Welcome story-teller from Earth!"

And she lived happily ever after on the space-station. After a long time, she visited both Earth and the Beta-planet, but that is a story for another day.

ACKNOWLEDGMENTS

I would like to thank P. Stuart Robinson, mentor, playwright, friend and professor, without whom this collection would still be in the future, and probably in another language altogether. His editing was exciting and challenging. *I like it, but don't you think it could have been a bit longer?* His belief that my stories could reach a wider audience was a wonderful encouragement.

Thank you: Catharina Schønning-Lykke for her enthusiastic reaction to my stories, her feedback and specific help in making sure I stopped editing in time.

Desmond Kinney for challenging me into writing more.

Brandon Sanderson's online lectures; The Writing Excuses podcast; the Writers of the future contest; Tromsø International Writer's workshop; WMG online workshops, particularly Kristine Kathryn Rusch; Helen and Mike Walters at Solus Or writing retreat; WORLDCON writers workshops. Thank you for providing an education and for your continued inspiration.

Science Fiction and Fantasy writers in Seattle and Iowa City.

To my father, Peter S. Lykke: For bringing me, first the world and then space, when he let me loose in his science fiction library.

Gro Berntsen, Therese Heimlund Lykke, and Nina Lykke for their support and for reading and commenting on early drafts over the years.

Thank you: My colleagues at "Stabburet- Verksted for ny litteratur", without whom I would still be editing and thinking I was alone with my writing.

Thank you Marlene Bruun Lauridsen for reading and finding more of the errors.

Thank you, friends, readers and writers I haven't mentioned because my mind was full of new stories, and my attention span and my bio-hard-drive needed expanding.

Thank you, my dear supportive husband: Ragnar Martin and my sons: Hauk-Morten, Harald and Henrik: For all your ideas, your laughter, your exhilarating questions and not the least: Your reading and your valuable input on any subjects medical, biological, mathematical, physical, mechanical, aerodynamical and lately even on Artificial Intelligence. Any remaining mistakes are my own.

Anitra H. Lykke, December, 2020

ABOUT THE AUTHOR

Anitra H. Lykke loves walking in the snow and lives comfortably in the arctic, with the occasional reindeer strolling by. She writes in several genres, but prefers science fiction. Her stories have been published in The Flash Fiction Press, and in Scandinavian magazines. One of her essays even won a prize in 2017. The Martian Vintage is her first collection of short stories.

Made in the USA
Columbia, SC
08 November 2022

70557937R00067